after

the

red

night

CHRISTIANE FRENETTE

after
the
red
night

a novel translated by
SHEILA FISCHMAN

Cormorant Books

Canada Council   Conseil des Arts
for the Arts   du Canada

The publisher gratefully acknowledges the support of the
Canada Council for the Arts and the Ontario Arts Council
for its publishing program. We acknowledge the financial support
of the Government of Canada through the Book Publishing
Industry Development Program (BPIDP) for our publishing activities.

Printed and bound in Canada

NATIONAL LIBRARY OF CANADA CATALOGUING IN PUBLICATION

Frenette, Christiane, 1954—
[Après la nuit rouge. English]
After the red night/Christiane Frenette; translated by Sheila Fischman.

Translation of: Après la nuit rouge.

ISBN 978-1-897151-14-3

1. Fischman, Sheila II. Title.

PS8561 R447 A8713 2009 C843'.54 C2009-900667-7

Cover design: Angel Guerra/Archetype
Interior text design: Tannice Goddard/Soul Oasis Networking
Author photograph © Dominique Thibodeau 2009
Printer: Transcontinental Printing

CORMORANT BOOKS INC.
215 SPADINA AVENUE, STUDIO 230, TORONTO, ON CANADA M5T 2C7
www.cormorantbooks.com

 Mixed Sources
Product group from well-managed
forests, controlled sources and
recycled wood or fiber
www.fsc.org Cert no. SW-COC-000952
© 1996 Forest Stewardship Council

that will be you the son come back in the night
the fairy tale someone
alien to love
[...]
I am already there in the mad unimaginable future
in lockstep with dread I walk on
among the stars that graced my birth and its
blindness

RACHEL LECLERC

MAY 1950

*T*hree days after the red night, Marie still hasn't come back to the house. The nuns at the convent hope that she, the best student in the class of 1949, would stay a while longer, to give them a hand. Since the hospice was evacuated on Saturday night, Marie has hardly slept. The first night she had spent inside the cathedral with the children. All terrified. The older children and the younger ones asked her if it was the end of the world. She had no reply.

Three days after the red night, Romain turns up at home with bag and baggage. His new life is beginning. At last. As soon as he arrives he goes to the scene. An entire district razed. Physicians — colleagues, he can say now — who'd come back from Europe when the war was over, had told him what they'd seen. Bombardments, villages set ablaze, destruction, hatred. Suddenly he felt as if he were there. Romain is speechless in the presence of people who search the rubble where their house had been. The slightest charred spoon found is a sign that life might go on.

Three days after the red night, Thomas still refuses to leave his room, despite the pleas of his parents. The nightmare is ending. Soon, men will come, they will calm their son with an injection, then take him away. Far. As far as Quebec City. Thomas is not like other young men. His parents have known that for a good while, but they hoped for a reversal of things, they cling to the idea that, with time, Thomas would find his way. He's not a bad boy, he doesn't bother anyone. Withdrawn, reserved, he only goes outside to walk his dog. In the evening or at night. On Saturday, though everything had keeled over, Thomas hadn't found his way, he had taken the emergency exit. Shortly after the fire broke out, he was pacing the streets, crying out to anyone who'd listen that it was he who had set fire to the Price Company lumberyard. Too busy, people paid no attention to him. At one point a man had ordered him to go home. Thomas had continued to proclaim his guilt. In the middle of the night, when the whole district was ablaze, he had begun to thrash about and to cry out in pain. He asked for help, claimed he'd been burned. His dog followed him, whimpering. Finally, his father found him and took him home. Since then, Thomas has been holed up in his room with his dog. He cut his sheets into long strips and wrapped them around his arms, legs, and chest. Now and then he howls. Outside his door, his father tells him again and again that there's nothing wrong with him, that there are no burns on his body. When he hears those words, Thomas howls even louder. Soon, men will come.

Three days after the red night, Joe is running home from school. Just time enough to change his clothes and grab his glove and his bat. He and his friends are to meet in a few minutes at the back of the vacant lot behind the hardware store. Some slightly older boys have challenged them. At this moment nothing exists for Joe but his will to win. Later this evening, before he goes to sleep, he thinks that he's just lived the most wonderful day of his life. Sinking into sleep, he murmurs that he's the best hitter in Joliet, Illinois.

Three days after the red night, Lou is not yet anything but a breath that is travelling towards the light. Three days after the red night, she has a premonition about the infinitesimal smell of ashes that reaches her when the greater part of her journey is behind her.

MAY 1955

"How could I forget it all?" Thomas wonders, his body given over to the swaying of the train, forehead pressed against the window, eyes staring vacantly. Over four years he had searched, tracked his memory, with no result. Then, gradually, bits had come back to him. The first time, the previous November, six months ago, he'd been working — pruning shrubs and burning leaves. He had raised his head abruptly and looked towards the St. Lawrence: the sun was going down, setting Lévis ablaze. Firelight. His dog had appeared to him then, in the middle of a fire. Panic-stricken, the animal was whimpering, with restraint, pathetically, as if he were forbidding himself to howl, to avoid rubbing it in. The dog, his whole body trembling, pressed himself against Thomas's legs. And that, in particular, is what Thomas remembers. So he was there too, in the nightmare.

That nightmare he knows by heart. How many times did his old psychiatrist tell him in detail about the red night? How many times has Thomas read the newspaper clippings that recount hour by hour how the fire had started and progressed? The doctor had brought them to him, saying: "Take a good look at the pictures too."Thomas had read and reread. He had examined every detail of the photos until his eyes were worn out. The gaping hole in the city, the burned-up part of the world, must resemble his brain. He couldn't remember a thing.

During his years in the hospital, people had told him over and over who he was and where he came from. That was how he'd learned that he had parents; that he was the only child of a respected Rimouski couple. Many of them — nurses, doctors, nuns — told him continually. They had spread the word: Thomas was intelligent, eventually the spark would appear. The young man made himself into the devil's advocate: "Your arguments aren't very sound," he told them. "If I had a father and a mother as you claim, they'd have come to see me here in the hospital ages ago!"The reply: "Rimouski is a long way from here, you know. Do you need proof, Thomas? Is there anything you lack? Cigarettes, for instance? Have you compared your clothes with those of the other residents? Your room may be tiny, but it's all your own, you can count on the fingers of one hand those who have one. Come on, we didn't invent your parents to ease your anxiety; your father exists, the proof is that he provides for you, provides for you very well. Now don't worry, you'll get your memory back."

They were right. Eventually, Thomas remembered. Not everything, but the essentials. Of his life, he had spliced together minute fragments and large sections; he had almost got back his childhood and adolescence, was even reconciled with the young man he had been during the year before the hospital. The fire was once more a personal memory that bore no resemblance to the newspaper accounts. He had reconstituted a nearly complete story, one that was plausible at any rate — his own. At night before he fell asleep, when he murmured his name he no longer felt like a stranger.

Thomas closes his eyes for a moment. The sun has disappeared behind the trees. He won't see it set. That will happen in less than an hour. His head is splitting. The usual pain. A while ago he had hoped that the coolness of the glass against his forehead would reduce the intensity. Not a day goes by without that pain coming to remind him that he has become a *hothead*. As a child he had been terrified of the word. His father had used it to talk about a gang of boys who one night had broken nearly all the windows in his warehouse. Thomas, who must have been five or six at the time, had imagined the worst. For one whole summer he had been afraid of coming across one of those boys with a healthy body and a charred head. The second memory that came back to him after the memory of the dog was this child's vision: those apocalyptic boys prowling around his father's warehouse.

Thomas rummages in the pockets of his jacket. Aspirins. He hates swallowing them without water. "Will there be someone at the station?" he wonders, without anxiety.

~⌒

EVERY NIGHT AT PRECISELY this time, Marie is exhausted. So worn out that she doesn't even feel her fatigue, her body shuts down, dissolves, as if to allow her to stay alive until evening is over. She wishes all her thoughts would disintegrate as well. Marie is finally alone. She put the children to bed earlier than usual. Romain will be home late. He's on an official assignment. One of his patients has asked if he will go with him to the station. His son is coming home after being away for five years. A childhood friend of Romain's. A complicated business involving a fake runaway and psychiatric internment. Romain seemed overwhelmed, something extremely rare, he is usually so stoical, whatever the circumstances. Marie pours herself a Scotch — a mortal sin, a man's drink — and collapses on the velvet sofa in the living room, which is never used. She fiddles with the crystal tumbler, a wedding present that's not used often either, that spends its life as a luxury object on display in the china cabinet in the living room, useless but so very chic.

Marie raises her arm and sets the glass precisely in the path of a ray of the setting sun. The regal colour of the Scotch, its heavenly taste, the sound of clinking ice cubes, the crystal, the mystery of the prism. Marie anticipates: in a moment, after just a few sips, the warmth will spread into the muscles of her arms and legs. Then into her head. And so the small fire of the Scotch will be enough to erase her thoughts. Marie will feel fine. Not for long — she won't have a second drink — but this pause will burn up all the beginnings of sentences that are jostling inside her and that always begin with: "I don't want." Marie sighs; the little fire is beginning its journey. Just as it arrives at her head, upstairs the baby starts to cry. Marie's muscles tighten. "I don't want any more children," she says, staring at her Scotch as if it were Romain.

The train is a few minutes late. Romain watches Thomas's father pace the platform, head sunk into his shoulders. In the car the man had begged him for help. He didn't know how things would develop, in what mood he and his wife would find their son. A five-year absence matters. Romain had promised, he wouldn't let them drop. In fact, it is Thomas whom he didn't want to let drop. Because of the incredible confession his parents had come to make in his office a few days earlier. Because of childhood. For Romain, Thomas represented something that had never existed: the kind of affection that's at the same time violent and carefree, that is born between children. Thomas. The escapades, the strong summer wind, the icy water of the river, catching snakes, the dreams, the perpetually skinned knees. Thomas from the house across the street, Thomas from elementary school, until life came between them. It had been far more than five years since he'd last seen him.

How many years? Romain counts. To begin with, there was the first separation around the age of fifteen or sixteen. Romain had gone to another college that his father considered more apt to train his son and make him worthy of his own ambition. Thomas had begun to isolate himself and had stopped going to school. His lack of interest — that was what had moved them away from each other, thinks Romain. Then, when he got it into his head to study medicine — or, rather, when his father had put the idea there — Thomas had withdrawn into a reality that no one comprehended at the time. He wanted to clear by himself a path that led nowhere. As for Romain, he swore by well-marked itineraries. For some years they only saw one another when Romain came home at the end of the school year. They were no longer in tune. And to punish Thomas for betraying their shared childhood, Romain played the card of superiority. He showed off to Thomas his new knowledge and the condescension that went with it. Then they hadn't seen one another again. Thomas had moved to the side of ignorance, Romain had stopped trying. And now he was the ignoramus, with his childhood and Thomas's laughter caught in his throat and blocking the way to the words that — as a good and empathetic doctor — he might speak to a father consumed with fear, who has just squeezed his arm at the sight of the train's headlights on the horizon.

As soon as the train begins to slow down, Thomas goes to the exit. At his feet, two travel bags. One is light: his clothes. The other, as heavy as if it were full of stones: his craft. Mainly treatises on botany, horticulture, truck farming, plus some small gardening tools. A craft he'd been taught in the hospital, then practised for two years in the gardens and greenhouses of the Plains of Abraham, which he has just left, driven by his memory that was eager to start all over again.

Thomas is calm. As you are after running away when you've gone as far as you can and want to come home. Neither hero nor victim. Nothing to prove, nothing to mourn. Only an appetite for life.

If there's no one to meet him, too bad, he'll go to a hotel. A room, four walls, that's something he knows. And then Thomas will walk, go to see what's become of the hole in the city facing the river, go to see with his own eyes what has been reborn from the burnt earth.

If he had it to do again, Thomas would act differently. He wouldn't send his parents a letter announcing that he was coming home. Nor would he phone to confirm the date and the time. This way of re-emerging had seemed natural to him: he was Thomas, he'd spent the first twenty-four years of his life here, in this city, surrounded by his parents. He was simply starting over where he'd left off. To the question about his family's five-year silence, he would oppose his own silence.

In fact, he had sensed that silence when his mother had choked on the telephone. The voice of Thomas. "Hello, Mama, it's me." She hadn't asked how he was, had stammered a few platitudes about his father and the weather. Thomas had sensed his mother's discomfort and had quickly moved on to the information about his arrival. She had said: "Wait, let me get a pencil." She's taking her own sweet time, Thomas had thought. Her voice had trembled when she asked him to repeat what he'd told her. He had complied, slowly, trying to put into his words the tenderness that sons feel for their mothers. She had ended the call, saying: "That's fine, Thomas, just fine, we'll be expecting you." She too had tried to put into her words the love that mothers feel for their sons.

MAY 2002

he last time I set foot in the Rimouski station, it wasn't to take the train. My father had decided to take my mother on a vacation. Except for their wedding trip, they had never gone away together. It was May, 1972, a few weeks after I turned sixteen, a kind of gift for that birthday. We were all there to see them off — my three brothers, my maternal grandparents, and me. The place impressed me: from there, one could go away. I was fascinated by the tracks that stretched out towards a mysterious elsewhere. My mother was nervous, she didn't stop complaining about the fact that to go to Europe, you first have to take the train to Montreal, then fly back over Rimouski — as if it weren't long enough already, seven hours in an airplane, seven long hours spent in a sardine tin wondering if the machine is in good condition, if a smoker will start a fire. My father looked at her with a vague smile, made no reply; he knew her, she would calm down eventually. A patient man, my father. He must have suggested this trip with the sole purpose of pleasing her, calming her. I'm not sure that he wanted to travel with her, I'm not sure that he even wanted to be with her. While my mother was getting worked up, my brothers and I stayed in the background. Each of us was appreciating in our own way the miracle that was happening: we four would be alone for two weeks. My brothers formed a homogeneous block; fewer than three years separated the eldest from the youngest. My father would tease them, call them the triplets, which they didn't mind at all; they were alike, well-behaved and studious, against the mode of the day. Their hair was clean and well-cut, they played sports, knew nothing of marijuana but the smell, didn't wear elephant jeans. My parents were leaving the family nest with complete peace of mind. As for me, no worry either, the wind wouldn't come up from my side, they believed. Even though I clashed with this fine family portrait with my long skirts, my hair and my necklaces à la Janis Joplin, in my own way I was just as well-behaved as my brothers, never saying one word louder than another, in fact, not saying much at all. I wasn't often at home, or if I was, I was in my room: "Your personality is strong but reserved, in spite of the way you dress," declared my mother. It was a point of view as good as any other. I myself would have said "unusual," yes, an unusual personality, maybe even a strange one.

At the time my mother was about the age I am today. I have an incredibly precise memory of every detail. I have the memory of an elephant.

I wish I had a photo of that moment. The last one that shows us all together. In any case, my mother was wearing a sleeveless pink dress. Kennedy pink, to be precise, she was obsessed with that colour ever since her idol's suit had been splashed with her husband's shattered brain. Her shoulder-length hair was impeccable, she'd just had it changed from dark brown to light, claiming that dark hair ages a woman's face — it's true, in fact I went blond myself a few years ago. Her shoes were woven white leather, with a matching purse that I thought was hideous. She didn't wear much makeup, only lipstick. Her eyes were very pale. At home, a few minutes before she left for the station, she had explained to me that one mustn't dress any old way for a plane trip. A matter of decorum. "Class is important in this life." That was her leitmotif, the basis of the education that she'd given us. She emphasized each word while spraying herself with her inevitable Chanel No. 5. Of course it was a way of saying that I didn't have any. "You and your hippie outfits," she would say. "You'll see, you'll tire of them, you're so young!"

If she saw me right now, would she notice that my stone-washed jeans have a designer's label? That my linen shirt, despite its ratty look, also has one. That the price of my Italian leather shoes and purse could feed every child in Eritrea for a good six months? Not to mention my jewellery. Would she think I'm dressed appropriately for a plane trip? I'm sure that I would disappoint her as much as Jackie did by marrying old Onassis and wandering around her Greek island with her hair blowing in the wind off the Mediterranean, dressed any old way. There won't be a reply. No one but the real estate agent will be waiting for me at the Mont-Joli airport.

My mother and father may be dead. As for my brothers, they most certainly must be living far from here. Life would have become unbearable after the trip to Europe. My mother will have given them a hard time. I didn't come back for them. Or for her.

I'm coming home, that's all. After a fugue state that lasted for what turned out to be thirty years.

If they were all there waiting to meet me at the airport, my mother in her pink dress, my so well-brought up brothers, I would plead guilty. But I'd be an unrepentant renegade. Ingratitude incarnate, yes, that's me.

To my mother's furious *why*'s I wouldn't know what to reply. I could only spout the empty formulas I've never allowed to enter my brain. *Running away means not wanting to wait*, people claim, or, if that truth doesn't fit the situation, one could also say, *refusing one's origins*. All right then, I didn't want to wait for life to burn me the way it burned my mother, I didn't want her distress. I didn't want her constantly repressed anger, or her indifference. Or waiting for her Kennedy pink and her Chanel No. 5 to contaminate me forever. Chalk it up to impatience. What's left is the matter of origin. Requiring a more complex explanation, dear shrinks. Yes, if running away means refusing one's origins, there was something to be refused that escaped me. It had something to do with instinct, with that need of mine to run away as soon as I could. I didn't recognize myself in the family portrait that was only attractive from the outside. Above all I didn't want to solve the mystery. In the civilized little tribe formed by the six of us, there was a wound so raw, so hot. My brothers didn't seem to feel it. My mother was standing, my father too. The ship was sailing. I swear that I haven't come back to end my days here, only to begin to navigate again.

"*N*o, no, I won't get up," thinks Marie, "he'll get back to sleep by himself." The sunbeam no longer strikes her glass. The sun has just set. What's left in the living room is a warm, diffuse light that makes objects and furniture look like the nave of a church. The baby won't stop. Marie stretches her legs, concentrates on her ankles, turning them, making them crack. Silence for a few seconds, then a nearly inaudible moan, a groan like that of a small animal dying alone, deep inside its hiding place.

Marie climbs the stairs four at a time. Yes, sure, if she has to ...

There is shit all over the crib. On the sheets, on the baby's pyjamas, in his hair. The smell. The child stops dying when he catches sight of his mother, and starts his siren again, deafening.

Marie's arms, her hands that without vexation, lay the baby on the changing table. Her confident movements, her face bent over the baby. Her third. Marie, her life, the dreams she didn't have, because girls have just one dream, bent over the baby as she gets ready to wipe. Marie, the envy of her convent friends, Marie, the handsome doctor, the lovely house, the lovely car, the lovely children.

An hour later she comes back down, feeling that the smell of shit has become embedded in her. Wherever she goes in the house, it's all she smells.

Darkness has fallen. In every room Marie switches on the lamps without thinking. She's furious: her evening has been taken away from her. She pours herself a second Scotch, a double, to burn the smell that pursues her. This time, she would like the small fire in her arms, her legs, and her head to resemble the red night.

Marie runs a bath, perfumes it, slips into it slowly, the drink in her hand. A moment later, she closes her eyes, she's been saved, the scent of lily of the valley joins that of Scotch, the shit smell is gone. Maybe everything, she thinks, begins and ends with an odour, and at the ultimate second of life that will be the ultimate observation. The smell of a candle, of a beloved body, of a disinfectant. Which one would she want at the moment of letting go? Are odours part of memory or of the nose? Which ones will have mattered to her? The first to resurface is the mixed odour of all the materials that make up the life of a city that's on fire: odours of wood, of textiles, of gasoline, of rubber, of hot metal. The odour of a night in May five years ago. The odour of her meeting with Romain a few days after the disaster in the cursed place. He was back sporting a stethoscope and his fine diploma. "Romain is going to set up his practice here," her mother had said proudly when she introduced them. Marie had quickly become part of that setting up. How could Romain be in love with her? Marie sometimes wondered. Most likely he loved her for her resourcefulness and her intelligence. That should be enough to make him settle here, thought Marie who, all things considered, was relieved that someone loved something about her. She who found nothing lovable about herself.

Marie gets out of the bath, dumps into it what's left of her Scotch. Definitely, after a certain amount, alcohol doesn't empty the head, but fills it. That was more than she'd asked for.

Wrapped snugly in a heavy old woolly bathrobe that she only parts with during summer heat waves, Marie checks out all the bedrooms. The two older ones are sleeping peacefully, each in his little iron bed, side by side. These boys are as much alike as two peas in a pod — the same eyes, same smile, as inseparable as twins. Tomorrow around six o'clock it is they, before the baby, who will sound the bugle. She doesn't go into the littlest one's room, but stands on the threshold, looks at him from a distance. Has seen enough for tonight.

Marie doesn't wait up for Romain. She falls asleep as soon as she lies down on her bed, protected from fire, cold, famine, lightning, and shit by the bathrobe she's worn since adolescence.

～〇

IN A CITY LIKE this it's not hard to find your way. Thomas is the first one off the train, a bag in either hand, followed by a few passengers. The train starts up again practically at once: Rimouski isn't the end of the world. Thomas walks peacefully towards his father. Who is that with him? he wonders.

As he gets closer, Romain senses the nervousness of the father at his side. Hears him murmur: "Don't worry, everything will be fine."

They shake hands. The father's first words: "Do you remember Romain? Your friend, our neighbour!" Thomas nods, his blue and candid eyes locked with Romain's. The truth is that Thomas does not remember. First shadow on the brain, vertigo, Thomas hopes that his friends won't be legion; he'd thought he had pieced together the entire puzzle.

Thomas and Romain, nearly the same age. One, his face emaciated, body long and lean, shoulders weary, seemingly dislocated, the slowness of his movements, the strange, supreme beauty emanating from him. An impression of dignity and sorrow. The other man, hair carefully combed, face fresh, flawless — he always shaves for a second time at the end of the day — the plump body of a well-fed man, holds his head and has a bearing that are surprising in one so young.

There they are, the three of them, exchanging platitudes. Now the father is more surprised than nervous. He thought that he would find a wild animal ready to tear him to pieces, while Thomas seems to have no redress to demand, no injustice to avenge. On the contrary, he moves around the set with obvious naturalness and detachment.

In Romain's car, Thomas does not speak. He has rolled

down the window. The city. The salt smell. The gaping hole no longer exists. Nothing shows; a new neighbourhood has emerged from the ashes of the one that once stood there. The place is unrecognizable.

"It's modern!" Thomas lets out. "I can't wait to see it up close."

"If you want we can come together, I'll explain about the reconstruction, the stages, all of it!" Romain hastens to reply.

Take the train. Come back home. Reconstruct each burned cell in his brain. It can't be explained.

In the house everything is still in its place. Another recovered memory that won't have betrayed Thomas. "Are you hungry? Thirsty? Would you like a piece of cake?" They are sitting at the kitchen table. Romain is still with them. A while ago the father insisted that he come in. A kind of official witness, or perhaps a mediator, Thomas thinks. How to not allude to the past five years?

His parents don't stop talking: the weather, the fishing season, the pneumonia that claimed the bishop last winter. They don't inquire about Thomas.

Nor does Thomas ask any questions, rather, *the* question. He doesn't need to, just seeing them he knows that he'll get his answer without having to open his mouth. Patience, patience, Thomas has learned, and anyway, does he really need that answer?

After an hour the atmosphere has relaxed, as if Thomas's parents were completely reassured: he's not delirious, or agitated, doesn't cry or drool. He is perfectly normal.

Thomas's headache, which had faded after he took the Aspirins, has come back with a vengeance. The coffee or the overly sweet cake or fatigue. "I think I'll lie down, it was a long trip." He stands up, takes his bags from the doorway, and makes his way leisurely but confidently to his room. Romain gets up too: "So long! I'll be in touch about checking out the city." Thomas doesn't reply. He is wrapped up in his little victory: his memory is speaking to him, leading him. At the end of the corridor, on the left, is the bathroom, on the right, his room: narrow, with a broad window that opens onto the yard, a tartan bedspread, a desk and its uncomfortable chair. His mother follows him: "Thomas …Thomas …" in a voice that tries to slow him down. Too late, he's already there, he found the switch instantly, without looking. Plodding memory, blessed memory.

His room has become a turquoise boudoir. Two white wicker chairs, a reading lamp, women's magazines. Lace at the window. And his bed, squeezed against a wall, which must have been brought up from the cellar in a hurry. With the tartan spread as a bonus. Thomas bursts out laughing.

"Look, Thomas, I'm sorry, I needed a little space of my own. I didn't think you'd come back, or no, that's not what I'm trying to say, I don't want to hurt your feelings, if I'd known …"

But she doesn't know, doesn't know a thing about sons who come home, doesn't know a thing about the unrelenting work of Thomas's memory, nor does she know that on scorched earth, bitterness can't germinate.

Alone at last. Thomas turns off the light and lies on the bed fully dressed. In this room, no odour to nourish his memory.

When Romain came home, he thought that Marie would be waiting for him. He looked in every room, and then a second time to turn off the lights. Intrigued — Marie didn't usually leave the lights on — he went upstairs. He saw her there, asleep, curled up in her old bathrobe, which he can't stand. He went to her, the alcohol on Marie's breath, slight but perceptible, made him step back.

He's not sleepy. His thoughts are filled with Thomas. He goes back downstairs, passes through the big, polished oak door that divides life in two: on one side, the house, Marie, the children; on the other, his office where every day he sees his patients. Romain searches in the files. When he moved here he bought the house from old Doctor Rhéaume, who was retiring. Along with the house came the office, the equipment, the patients. Many had changed doctors. One does not move naturally from an experienced doctor to a young one barely out of medical school. But all the inactive files were still asleep, intact, carefully arranged in case the patients came back. Tonight, Romain wants to know if Thomas is sleeping somewhere between two files. He only finds that of his parents.

*C*hicago–Toronto, Toronto–Montreal, Montreal–Quebec City, Quebec City–Mont-Joli. With each flight the plane has been smaller. It's no longer possible to take a plane without a suspicious look at the other passengers. As soon as a raised voice or an overly emphatic laugh is heard, heads turn abruptly, and for a fraction of a second an end-of-the-world terror passes through everyone's eyes. Most people hate flights like this one: tiny planes multiply tenfold the feeling of insecurity. I, though, quite like them. Besides, today, of the twenty seats, only nine are occupied. No one beside me. The chance of terrorists on board is nil. Unless the FLQ is active again ... When the Internet arrived a few years ago, Joe sat me down in front of the screen and said: "Watch! The world is coming to you, and the past as well!" Before my eyes streamed the front pages of newspapers: *La Presse*, *Le Devoir*, *Le Soleil*. "Now try to resist!" Joe has never understood that one can close a book and never want to open it again. For him, things should always be in movement — including U-turns and backing up. I shrugged as I asked him what he was playing, if he really thought that I was going to torment myself, that I was going to challenge my very existence because

I'd read all those front pages. He laughed, telling me that he would bet heavily on it. He was mistaken. It wouldn't be enough to stir anything in me.

He's the only person who has ever really mattered. Joe is *mon Amérique à moi*. It was as if he was waiting for me that morning when I arrived at the bus terminal in Toronto. I'd been travelling for more than twelve hours, curled up at the back of the bus, shoulders hunched for fear that someone would recognize me, arrest me, and send me home. My heart was pounding, as if I'd run from Rimouski to Toronto. And I hadn't eaten for more than twelve hours. I must have looked like a starving animal; there was nothing of the big bad wolf about him when I accepted his invitation to have breakfast at the restaurant in the terminal. Today such a picture would look obscene: a thirtysomething male approaching a teenage girl in a bus terminal. But the time lent itself to it; the belief was that salvation would come from friendliness. Refusing to speak to a stranger fell under decadence, except for my mother. Joe came across as something of a cowboy. He gobbled his two eggs, bacon, and sausages in no time. He was in the import–export business. He'd come to Toronto looking for merchandise. He was going directly back to Chicago with a stop in Detroit. He owned a van. I could come along if I wanted. I haven't disembarked since. His plans were simple: make a lot of money, travel, and not have children. He saw us set for life, I just had to acquiesce. He was in love. Children didn't matter to me, travelling did though, and as for money, I couldn't have cared less. If he wanted it that badly, it was his business. Joe was holding the pistol, his finger in position on the trigger. I said yes and the starting signal rang out all over America.

homas woke up at dawn, as usual. This morning the ritual to which he had submitted for two years won't be observed. He won't go down to his landlady's kitchen for breakfast; won't listen to her complaints about the man on the third floor who came home at dawn drunk again, waking everyone except Thomas, who still had, from his years in the hospital, the ability to enclose himself like an oyster, asleep or awake. Thomas is the old lady's favourite. Quiet, hard-working, obliging. If only he were more talkative ... After breakfast Thomas will not walk into the emerging sunlight to join his squad of gardeners for another day's war against insects, weeds, and grass that needs to be cut.

Here, in his childhood room, time seems suspended. The minutes, the seconds when body and mind work at belonging only to the present moment, aren't here yet. They will come or they won't. Thomas doesn't know. There's no rush. Today, it's his memory that is directing the delicate operation of securing the present to the past.

Thomas feels like walking to the burned neighbourhood. As soon as he sticks his nose outside, the smell of seaweed and sandbar hits him brutally. Change of program, head for the St. Lawrence, instinctively.

The day will be fine and mild. Thomas walks slowly, hands in his pockets, his big body, his ruined shoulders. Think of nothing. He lets his gaze wander to the river, doesn't realize that he has turned off to the right and is now heading for his father's warehouses. As a child, Thomas had dreamed about working there but the darkness of the place, the grease, the smell of rubber, his father's voice had soon convinced him otherwise. When Thomas realizes where he is heading, he speeds up. It's a matter of checking. Will the warehouses be the same as the ones that his memory has restored to him?

They are the same, but faded and worn, the big, multi-paned windows are dirty, opaque, the paint peeling. At this hour the employees are not yet at work. Backed onto the warehouses as an annex is the shop and, above the door, the sign with his father's name, also faded and worn, in the image of the rest. Some day, thinks Thomas, nothing will be left of all that, someone will come, offer a ridiculous sum for the buildings, his father will have aged, he'll say yes. The bulldozer will do the job in a matter of minutes. A house of cards brought down.

Thomas continues his inspection of the premises, circles the rusty machinery left lying around, which gives the impression that it hasn't been all that long since the bulldozer restored some innocence to the place. Behind the shop, near where scrap of all kinds is piled up, Thomas notices what looks like a kennel — a bunch of boards nailed together in a slapdash way, leaving big cracks — and right next to it, a dog on a chain is asleep, curled up in a ball. Surprised that the animal hasn't noticed him, Thomas approaches. The dog isn't aware of the sound of footsteps on the pebbles, or of the tall, weary young man walking towards him with tears in his eyes, like someone advancing towards the promised land. Thomas's dog. A gift from his parents in an attempt to break open the cage in which he'd shut himself away. The animal hadn't let the young man out of his sight and had immediately joined his life to Thomas's dread until the two were one: the red night.

Thomas is very close to him, crouching. The animal finally reacts. "Do you recognize me, old pal?" The dog searches with his muzzle. His eyes are dull; Thomas realizes that he can't see. He can't hear either, Thomas hasn't grasped that yet. He has recognized his master's odour; he rushes towards Thomas, bumps into him. His whole body trembles. The promised land, the memory of dogs.

Excited, he jumps onto Thomas, nearly knocks him over, shoves him to one side, licks him. Thomas pets the dog, grabs him by the scruff of the neck, tugs at his ears, his tail. Rediscovered games. The dog answers, nibbles at the man's clothes.

The animal is in a pitiful state: skinny, dirty, coat dull and tangled.

Gradually, he calms down. Thomas holds the dog's head in his hands. "I can't believe how badly you've been treated.

You'll see though, you and I, we're going to start over, I promise." And Thomas begins to sob because he no longer believed. Because yes, it did happen, something violent that's not in his memory has just assailed him, has snatched him from the torpor that serves him as certainty. Something furious and thrilling. Something as powerful as anguish or fear, but their opposite. That does not separate but brings together. A sensation of such intensity. Even more than the dread triggered by the shock treatments.

A moment later Thomas gets to his feet, rubs the dust off his clothes. "Come, Rex, it's over, I'm taking you home." He unfastens the dog. Oh, the definitive sound of the chain that Thomas threw against the shop's sheet-metal wall with all his might.

The din has attracted the attention of an employee who has just gone into the shop. Seeing Thomas walk away with the dog at his heels, he runs and shouts: "Hey, you! Where do you think you're going?" Thomas stops, so does the dog. He's very young, sixteen or seventeen at most.

"What're you doing with that dog?"

There's something aggressive in the eyes and voice of the boy who has just found a golden opportunity to get rid of him: a dog thief!

"I came to get my dog," Thomas replies calmly.

"Your dog! Yeah, sure. You and who else!"

"See that sign? Edmond Garant is your boss, yes or no?"

"Yes," replies the young man, who's becoming suspicious

of Thomas, of his strange blue eyes, of his drawling voice.

"Edmond Garant and Son, and that's me."

"There's no *Son* on the sign," replies the young man belligerently.

"And there never will be either! But don't trust appearances!" shouts Thomas, who's back on the road, the dog sticking to him like his shadow.

I more or less understood what import–export meant when Joe placed in my hands a Canadian passport in my name with a false birthplace — I'd become a Montrealer — and a falsified birthdate. He had made me five years older; all at once I was of age. That way, he said, we could get married, I would acquire another name, papers, and an American passport. We could travel. With no problems. That suited me fine — exit the runaway girl — I would lose the reflex of always checking every street corner, every business, every park, to be sure that my mother wouldn't suddenly appear, with handcuffs and straitjacket, to take me back to Rimouski. To seal my new identity, I went to a hairdresser for the first time in my life, I had my hair cut — exit Janis — I used makeup to earn those five more years, and I went to a photographer for the passport shots. Once I had them all in hand, I was amazed: I had the impression that I was looking at my mother. Her hair, her nose, her uptight little smile. But not the eyes. Hers were very beautiful, pale grey, mine were blue, too big, almond-shaped, but in reverse.

We got married shortly afterwards. It rained cats and

dogs that day, Joe had assembled some of his few friends, all men of his age except for a young woman who spoke neither English nor French. Ceremony in hasty mode. At six o'clock we were home in time for supper. It was not until that precise moment, when we were inside Joe's messy apartment, that I really understood that the rocket, which had dropped me on Mars, had just taken off again, destination Earth.

Joe was happy. That was blindingly obvious. It didn't make me want to come back to Earth.

The good thing about the beginning of love is that you don't need to think. We were there, together, totally isolated on our planet, we were there in the light, in our silences and our words. Money came flooding in — the import–export business may have been some kind of scam, I didn't want to know — I drew, I watered my plants. The shade wasn't interested in us, so we lived our lives as if it didn't exist, we went on, blinded by all the light, accomplishing our little deeds, pointless but so alive.

My life was progressing according to the script as planned. We travelled. I didn't follow Joe every time he went away. South America enchanted me, I learned Spanish, I never missed an opportunity to go there. Neither Joe nor I felt "the call of the race" in our bellies, the will not to have children still held. I got used to my new name: Lou Thompson. Lou is the diminutive of Louise. It was Joe who'd started to call me that. Today, no one knows that my first name is Louise. My mother chose it because of her favourite flowers. That garden of hers! It seemed more important to her than her children. It was vast, it lined two streets, and drew admiring looks from passersby. "A source of pride for the city," the mayor had declared one day when he presented her with a small souvenir plaque. In this garden there were far more phlox than any other variety of flower. They were in every colour and every height. My mother made bouquets of them. When they were in bloom the house resembled a funeral parlour. She never called them by their official names, she said "my Louises" the way she said "my Saint Josephs" for her petunias.

Then one day, calmly, we began to think again. I put my drawings in a binder and took them to show to some people sitting behind big desks, whose mahogany colour recalled my father's. I used to sit there often to draw, it was peaceful, my father had deserted the place when he started working at the hospital, and most important, my brothers didn't bother me there. I became an illustrator. I worked at home. Joe was so proud that he bought a bigger, more luxurious apartment so that I could have an office in keeping with my talent, as he said. I saw no one, I worked hard. Drawing took on a different meaning. I was happy. I felt as if I were sheltered from everything. In a sense I was still the little runaway who was constantly in hiding. I never thought about them. Never did their faces make their way to me. The door was locked. I'd thrown away the key. Finding it was without a doubt the greatest threat hanging over my life. I'd realized that once when I was drawing phlox for a gardening book.

Eventually, flowers and plants became my specialty. My work had been noticed. The garden was enlarged: I drew flowers for fabrics, wallpaper, tablecloths, curtains. Modern or classic, depending on the order, while I scrupulously respected the colours in fashion. Joe joked: "You're the best gardener without a garden!"

With spring, the light seeps into the bedrooms earlier, despite the opaque curtains. The children adjust to the rhythm of the day. Marie goes down the stairs cautiously, in her left arm she holds the baby against her, in her right hand she is holding that of the younger son, the older one follows them, leaning against the wall. The tribe. Today, Marie will be able to catch her breath. Yvonne, the cleaning lady, will be coming. Marie will have some time. During the afternoon while the children are having their nap, she will be totally free: no cooking, no housework, she'll even be able to go out if she feels like it. For the time being though she can't even think about it, the day is getting underway right now. The baby has started to cry, he's hungry. Marie can't give him his bottle until the other two have begun to eat: they're starving too, are showing their impatience. Everything has to be done at the same time: bottle, cereal, toast. First step: orange juice to busy the mouths of the older ones. Marie would sell her soul for a sip of coffee right now. The toast is burning, the eldest pours his orange juice onto the youngest. The kitchen is transformed into an arena. The clamour, the lions, the poor Christians in the middle. This is the moment that Spartacus chooses to save her. Romain, in pyjamas but already shaved, kisses her neck. "Go feed the baby in the living room." Before he even finishes his sentence, Marie has disappeared with the baby.

The father's voice. The children fall silent. Already, at the ages of three and eighteen months, they understand that the world of men and the world of women are separate. They wait quietly for Romain to feed them. Unlike Marie, Romain talks all the time. That's how he is. He explains things to them in detail: why they mustn't cry, they must be reasonable, they're older, their mama doesn't like it when they quarrel at mealtime. He speaks to them like a doctor explaining to a patient the nature and the consequences of his illness in terms that the patient doesn't comprehend. For the children listen, fascinated, without understanding what he's carrying on about. What they like, what they recognize in this goggledygook is the complicity, the exclusive nature of a way of talking, of a world that they belong to. "We get along well, don't we, guys?" Romain concludes, as he sets a coloured plate in front of each of them. Being men together, already.

Marie comes back to the kitchen; the peace treaty with their stomachs has been signed. The baby is playing in his playpen, the other two in the corridor. It's her turn now to have breakfast. Romain follows her with his eyes, saying nothing. What can he do for Marie? What can he say to her? For her, an unforgivable lack of concern, for him a most acceptable stroke of bad luck. Three children so close together is still better than sterility. It's not a trivial matter, being there together, in good health, with the certainty of a future without loneliness, even though the present seems overpopulated.

"You smelled of alcohol last night," Romain tells her when she joins him at the table. Oh, he would like to use the proper tone of voice — somewhat offended, somewhat let down — but Marie's mood this morning doesn't lend itself to that. In this town, people know the power of a spark.

"I'd rather smell of alcohol than shit!" replies Marie, who obviously doesn't feel that she's been caught red-handed.

"And what exactly was it you were drinking?"

"Scotch."

"Scotch!" says Romain, surprised. "You like Scotch?"

"Yes, I like Scotch. I like to hold a glass of Scotch in my hands, in the evening, when the children are in bed and I'm alone, when I'm so tired I can't take it anymore. Tell me, Doctor, is there something wrong with that? Am I going to come down with cancer, hepatitis, or multiple sclerosis if I have a Scotch now and then when I'm exhausted?"

Romain does not reply, congratulates himself on having gone easy with her.

If Marie can count on Yvonne to make her life easier and keep her informed about all the gossip and rumours in town, Romain too has a faithful accomplice — his secretary, who has become more attached to him, more quickly, than she had to Doctor Rhéaume, for whom she worked over thirty years. The only tasks she can't perform in his office are diagnoses, and even that … There is nothing she doesn't know about dressings, dosages, reading blood pressure.

Every day of the week, including Saturday, she arrives at 7:00 a.m., two hours before the first patient, one hour before Romain. When he shows up everything is flawlessly in place: the files for the day, reports of examinations, patients to call back. Madame Beaurivage, Romain's memory. But even more, the memory of a good part of the town: thirty-five years of secrets, of rifts, of births, of disgraces, of suffering and death recorded more effectively in her than in the wall of filing cabinets behind his desk.

She rules supreme over the administration of this office, having for thirty years applied rules that had made Romain cringe when he first settled here. Then he had imposed his own authority. Authority that Madame Beaurivage recognized in everything except where his fees were concerned. For the young doctor fresh out of medical school, rates were some-thing to be set in advance according to the complexity of the work done — vaccinating a tiny baby required more dexterity than scribbling a prescription. For Madame Beaurivage though that was not the prevailing logic. Hers was simple: she had always applied it during the days of Doctor Rhéaume, and she intended to do the same with Romain. Actually, Madame Beaurivage felt that the charge should be based on the patient's ability to pay. Clearly put, the richer the patient, the more he paid; the poorer, the less. Simple and fair.

"It's what every doctor in the world has always done!" she had exclaimed indignantly to Romain.

"Yes, Madame Beaurivage, but this isn't the nineteenth century, it's 1955! I suppose you're going to tell me that a farmer can pay me with cream and butter or a leg of pork? And what do you do when a patient comes for the first time and you don't know him from Adam?" asked Romain, convinced that he'd found the flaw in the system.

Madame Beaurivage had looked at him as if he were the last of the gullible fools.

"You can tell everything about a person from the clothes on their backs."

Romain had given in even though he disagreed, telling Madame Beaurivage that the situation would be changing very soon. He never mentioned it again. After such a forceful introduction, things had gone smoothly. They were fond of one another.

This morning, Madame Beaurivage is humming to herself as usual while she prepares for the day. From the other side of the wall, she can hear the morning concert. A deafening mixture of tears and squeals. When the polished oak door opens at eight o'clock, she calls to Romain without even looking up to say good morning: "Do you know what your wife could use, Doctor? A live-in maid. Yvonne has mentioned several times that she'd give up her other clients if you asked her. In fact her fondest hope is to work just for you and your family. I think she's become very attached to the children. And her own life is so sad, with her mother who's always suffering but never sick ... That's one who pushes her luck! Yvonne's mother should be in an old folks' home, and so should Yvonne! That would be the perfect solution for everyone!"

"I wish I had your ability to settle the problems of the world! But it's not that simple, Marie won't hear of it. She maintains that she couldn't stand to have a woman's eyes on her all day long."

"A maid wouldn't have one second free to have her eyes on your wife."

"I know, but Marie is Marie."

The office doorbell cut short their conversation. Madame Beaurivage grumbles: "Hey, not so early, not for another hour."

It's not a patient, it's Thomas's father, and he urgently wants to have a word with the doctor. He's nervous again as he was at the station. Romain shows him into his office.

"Now what do we do?" he asks, as if Romain had just told him that his cancer is spreading faster than anticipated.

"What exactly do you mean, Monsieur Garant?"

"Look, at six o'clock this morning he'd already gone out."

"So?"

"So, so — what am I supposed to say to people? And even more, what's *he* going to say? I don't want them thinking I'm crazy!"

"Crazy to whom? Thomas or other people?" Romain replies. "I think what's most important is to clear things up with

Thomas. You owe him the truth. In fact, the matter should be settled by now."

"The simplest thing would be if I told him to drop in and see you. You could do it better than me, doctors are used to it, and besides, he's not your son, it would be easy for you. And at the same time you could ask him if he intends to stay."

"Would it bother you if he doesn't leave again?"

"Depends. He'd have to behave."

"Okay, fine, I'll talk to him," Romain concludes with a sigh.

*T*ime has passed; nearly thirty years in the arms of a cowboy in the middle of a garden that has never existed. And then one morning less than a year ago, things changed radically. We said goodbye, as if we wouldn't see each other again until that evening, even though my office and his are at either end of the same corridor. I was in a hurry; I was behind in my work. Joe smiled at me. I stopped for a minute to look at him in his worn jeans, his torn sweatshirt; he was flooded by light, he hadn't shaved for two days — as is often the case since he's been working more at home — I was struck by the uniform white of his new beard. He's getting older. He made the first move, as usual. To protect me, so that when my turn comes I would know where to place my feet so as not to sink too abruptly into the swamp. My father's face crossed my mind briefly. I thought that he must be a very old man now and that I'd never seen him unshaven; perfectly smooth skin was an obsession for him.

Eyes narrowed because of the sun, he raised his cup of coffee as if he were drinking a toast to the day. Then he collapsed.

The doors of the ER closed behind the stretcher that was carrying him away. I was standing behind those doors, lost, cut off from the entire universe, unable to move, to shout, to cry. A nurse came back and took me through the doors. I stepped into a war zone just after the fighting has stopped. The medical staff ran from one room to another, shouting orders. Joe was not the only one to have fallen on the battle-field that morning. I was taken to a tiny room that opened onto the main corridor. Three or four chairs fastened together, a small, low table, some old magazines. Perhaps others came to wait there too, I saw nothing. Six hours later I sensed a presence at my side. "Mrs. Thompson?" From the doctor's nervous voice, I knew at once that Joe was alive. "Let me explain," he said, trying to speak more slowly. He used technical language as if he were talking to a colleague. He stared at the wall behind me. I brought my hand to my neck. He looked at me and was silent for a moment. He resumed his explanation. It took just a few words: Joe had suffered a burst aneurysm.

Three surgeries, a month-long coma, six months of inten-sive rehab; months of telling me again and again that he would blow his brains out as soon as he was able. Then he calmed down a little. The after-effects: paralysis of the right side, speech difficulties, slight vision problems, and me. He would not end it all. He would be enraged for the rest of his life, but he wouldn't leave me all alone. He had announced it to me in one sentence: "We should have had children."

Everything became too big for me — the apartment, the fantastic light that pours into it, Chicago, America. Everything became too cramped for him: his body, the apartment. He no longer wanted to go outside.

I too had an urge to end it all: on a sudden impulse, without thinking it over for a second, I put forward the idea of life in a white house on the bank of a great river far away.

The tone in which I delivered my plans was so dictatorial, so ridiculous, that knowing us, there should have been a few brief seconds of silence, silence in the form of a question: "Oh, a stroke?" followed by a shared burst of laughter. Instead, Joe simply responded with a sigh that spoke eloquently about what he anticipated for himself, for us. "Whatever you want, baby."

I had lost him. I had lost the man who loved the din of the world. And all I came up with to offer him was to go away. I wanted it to be my turn, I wanted to give back to him what he'd given me. I was suggesting that we run away again, with everything that implied by way of adventures and fresh starts. He listened to me. I understood what he left unsaid: the white house on the bank of a great river that I'd talked about he saw not as a new beginning, but as an internment. Still, he said yes with a hopeless tenderness that tore me apart: a man who felt as if his body was a place of internment still needed a place.

Now and then I tried the strong method: "Stop wallowing in self-pity, you could have been a quadriplegic. You can walk, you're alive!" His reply was to tighten his grip on the support bar of his walker.

It was not the most brilliant idea, I know, but I hadn't found any other. I had taken the reins. He was not strong enough to argue. I didn't know the source of that drive or what sleeping gene had wakened in me. For reassurance, I kept telling myself that I was not mistaken: any animal in danger dreams of the hole where it was born. That image of a creature fleeing towards its birthplace while supporting his damaged love would become my mantra. Most important, it must not be allowed to lag behind. Now, as we are living in an age when nothing is left to drag along, what came next got underway at lightning speed. I visited houses sitting in front of my screen. I retained a few that must have been unsaleable, they were so expensive. In the face of my insistence, Joe finally visited them too. "Whatever you want, baby." I asked Mark, our neighbour's grandson and star quarterback of his college team, to move in while I was away.

"A bodyguard? I can manage on my own!" Joe protested.

"I can't."

I packed my bags. Joe watched me, leaning against the doorway of our bedroom.

"Usually it was me …"

I didn't reply, he went on: "One day you left everything behind. I took it calmly. You're still young, Lou! Do it again! Now! Do it for me!"

There are so many ways to say things. I took it calmly. I

was at the shoes. I was trying to choose — I always pack too many when I travel. A moment later when I turned towards him, he hadn't budged either. His face was strained. In his eyes, a shadow that I didn't recognize. His courage was unbearable, indispensable to me.

I will not be at peace until we're in that house. Though I've taken drastic measures to ensure that he won't be left by himself for even a moment, before I've exited the plane I'm already eaten up with worry.

Finally, we land. In the tiny airport the real estate agent who's waiting for me must be already rubbing his hands. *Big deal!* Here comes the rich American with her big bucks! None of the people I've spoken to is aware that I speak French. Which is fine. For transactions. And emotions.

*N*ow life can continue, thinks Thomas, after he spends part of the morning hanging out on the bank of the St. Lawrence River. It's the first time he has really thought that. They'd tried to persuade him to do so when he left the hospital, to reassure him, encourage him to plunge to the heart of the world. They didn't tell him, however, that his life would go on; rather, that he would start it over from scratch. A slight difference. Today, for instance, he hasn't started anything over. It was life that took the lead. Life that was first to throw the dice. That placed the shifting light above the river, that, as the sun warmed the shore, raised the odour of mud and salt, and the ragged cries of sea birds. And it is life that has given back the riverbed to Rex, and Rex to Thomas. That has placed in their canine and their human lungs bursts of air or of happiness, neither of them knows which. This morning, life is as wide as the river.

Noon. Thomas is starving. So is Rex. They quicken their pace towards the house. When they cross a street, Thomas bends down and lays his hand gently on the dog's back. Because of cars. Even if there are none on most of the streets they take.

Every day, the father comes home to eat. Half an hour later he leaves again. The mother listens to the radio while she does the dishes, then disappears into her bedroom for a nap. Unchanging ritual. When Thomas comes in, leaving him on the front steps, Rex moans. Thomas gestures to him to wait. Pointless, Rex can't see. He takes off his muddy shoes and picks up the plate that his mother has left on the counter for him. "Rex," he says, all smiles. His father doesn't want to know any more, he goes back to work without finishing his meal.

The afternoon doesn't contradict the morning. Thomas settles in. While his mother was sleeping, he gave her back her boudoir. He moved his bed down to the cellar, positioned it near the window. The tartan bedspread, folded in four, on the cement floor. Rex. He took the big steel basin into the yard, washed his dog. "Good dog," he told him as he was rubbing him dry.

His mother has gone out to join him: "But Thomas, the boudoir, your room, your bed in the cellar — it makes no sense!"

She never says a complete sentence, only truncated bits, punctuated by her nervous, wheezy breathing. Has she always been like that? Thomas wonders.

"Seriously, Thomas, what's got into you? Are you crazy?"

Too late, the word is out, she turns crimson.

"Do you really expect an answer?" Thomas replies, scornful, in his drawling voice.

Some days ought to disappear, crumble into dust as soon as they begin. They carry a curse, a calamity that can be observed all around: in children's babbling, in Marie's unruly hair, in the dark circles under her eyes, in the dingy images in her mirror. Even in Yvonne's smile and her eagerness to share the latest news gleaned at the grocery store. On a day like this, no matter what you do or where you are or where you go, you are still a total stranger, you speak an incomprehensible language, whatever you do seems to be impeded by heavy chains.

When those days coincide with Yvonne's arrival, Marie is enraged. The day will be wasted when it should have been advantageous. She takes refuge in silence in her "office," as Romain has dubbed it — the sewing room that's indispensable to any good housewife, said the nuns at the convent who had moreover given their pupils various drawings, plans modelled on the premises, with illustrations of equipment, furniture, and utilitarian objects. The drawings also showed women busy at noble tasks: embroidering, mending, knitting. Their hair was nicely done, they were well-dressed, in their Sunday best actually. They smiled. The pupils dreamed.

Marie though no longer dreams. Her sewing room is undoubtedly more attractive, better equipped than those imagined by the nuns, for Romain had been generous. He is a doctor who is fascinated by the coming technological revolution, always ready to invest in a new instrument or in new state-of-the-art specialized devices. He had that reflex about everything. And so Marie too found herself working in an ultramodern office.

In the very early days of their marriage, Marie had launched herself frenetically into sewing. So much needed doing to brighten up this austere house. A regime change was needed, that of Doctor Rhéaume and his family, which had lasted forty years, had to be brought to an end. Marie had been proud when she moved into this plush house that exuded so much dignity, but on the other hand, she'd been alarmed by its nooks and crannies, its dark wallpaper and woodwork, by the permanent odour that she described as cabbage soup, which got a laugh from Romain, who in this house only breathed the odour of Marie, her female odour in his house.

They had married in March, off-season, joked Romain, who had opened his practice some months before and who saw more advantages to celebrating this wedding at the end of winter than in waiting, as Marie would have liked, for the spring. Lilacs, birds, light wedding gowns were no match for his arguments: Marie in his life, in his bed, right away.

They'd gone away for just a brief honeymoon — where could they go in March? Romain had taken Marie to Quebec City. She had never been out of Rimouski, he'd shown her around the Quartier Latin, his home base during medical school, had taken her to sleep in the Château Frontenac, and to walk in the dirty, wet snow. Marie was thrilled. Quebec City was wonderful, and Romain had proved to be worthy of his profession: he knew what to do with a human body. But no more than she had before their marriage, Marie could not persuade herself that Romain was really in love: he was only lenient, the young man remained an enigma — he had so many choices and such an ordinary young wife.

They'd gone back to Rimouski, real life had begun. Marie worked with a will. A question of not disappointing. She wanted Romain to see her the way people saw him. With the deference and admiration conferred by the indispensable work of caring for and mending bodies.

Yes, real life. Early in the morning, Romain walked through the polished oak door, generally didn't eat at noon, and didn't walk through the door again until supper time. Often he went back and spent part of the evening in his office, consulting files. Of course, she told herself, there aren't just good sides to marrying a doctor. It was not Romain's physical absence, her solitude as a young wife in a house designed for eight children, that had surprised her at first, no, it was Romain's absence, period, his way of not noticing what characterized, what constituted life to the west of the polished oak door: Marie's domestic and culinary exploits, her efforts — it took up all her time! — to make this house reflect them. Marie was disappointed. With herself. How had she been able to keep alive in her the dreamy, naive student who came first in class, with honourable mention in the domestic arts? Everything she did was ridiculous; Romain, at every minute of his day, was busy saving humanity. How could she resent his not noticing the embroidered curtains in the kitchen? Then again, Marie faced facts: for Romain there weren't two lives, only one, as if the oak door stayed permanently open; he exerted on her the same benevolent authority as on his patients.

Quite coincidentally, the sewing room and Romain's examining room were contiguous. While all the other rooms were absolutely soundproof, those two were not: the wall between them had been added long after the house was built, probably without paying too much attention to the choice of materials. Marie can hear indistinct voices rise up in a murmur. To her great relief though, the words, the conversations are inaudible. Still, when a child cries or a woman sobs, their suffering passes through the wall as if it were paper. In the early days of their marriage, that had moved her. She was a witness in a way. Perhaps more useful than she thought.

Five years later, the sounds no longer move her: they irritate her, exasperate her. As if there could never be silence in her own world. As if there was no end to their demanding that he restore the grace of their bodies. The impossible. As if they expected everything from Romain, asked for and obtained everything. Sometimes, rarely, bursts of Romain's laughter came to her. Unbearable.

Today, the sounds from the examining room seem ten times louder. Abrupt sounds, sounds of metal on metal, as if Romain is dropping everything he puts in his hands. And then all those babies baying at the moon, while her own have finally gone to sleep for part of the afternoon. Marie has shut the door so that Yvonne won't disturb her. In a moment the drone of the sewing machine will cover the relentless voices that are seeking salvation beyond the examining room. Will cover as well the fierce voice that is seeking its salvation beyond the sewing room.

T've bought a house on the river, away from the city. It will be ready in August. That gives us three months to leave Chicago. I asked for it to be painted white. The architect is surprised: the last owners had just painted it. No, not blue, I promised Joe that it would be white. For the interior I asked to have the doorways widened, the bathrooms enlarged, the nooks and crannies eliminated. I had taken care before leaving to measure the width of Joe's walker; I couldn't bear it if he had to struggle with space. I even had an elevator installed.

I took piles of photos for Joe. In the plane that's taking me back to Chicago, I feel light, relieved. I know it sounds crazy, but I feel hopeful. As if it were possible to start everything anew.

Mission accomplished, I passed the first test. Except for some palpitations at the sight of the river, I didn't lapse into pathos. I turned down the real estate agent's offer to show me around town, I even changed the subject abruptly when he started to tell me about the fire in 1950. My thoughts were limited to this house, Joe, me, to the future that might be totally insane. I played my part wonderfully well, at certain moments it frightened me: yes, that was me, the rather affected Mrs. Thompson who felt just fine in front of the notary, the real estate agent, the architect, and other temple merchants. I resisted the images that were assaulting me: myself as a child running in my mother's garden, and then, shortly afterwards, myself in my father's office, crying my eyes out when he disinfects my knee. I've also resisted the assaults of the present: I haven't opened the telephone book that sits prominently on the small table in my hotel room. I haven't tried to find the addresses of my ghosts.

The second test is harder: to go back to Chicago, to the house, see Joe again after a week-long absence, during which I tried hard to conquer a new kingdom for him. To see again his defeated face when I place at his feet the biggest haul that I was able to bring back. No one in the apartment. There's a certain disorder, the ashtrays are full, I hate the smell that goes with it. Joe has left me a note: "Don't panic, I haven't disappeared, I'm at physio till five." I let myself collapse onto the living-room sofa. Close my eyes. Suddenly, dizziness, amnesia. To go home: I don't know where or how I unlearned that.

At five on the dot Joe is there, followed by his young bodyguard. I wake up with a start. Hear his voice calling me from the hall. His former voice. The voice that talks too fast and too loud, that shoves everything aside to make itself heard. He's just been told that if he continues to make such good progress, soon he won't need his walker, just a cane.

Again, the hope of starting over. Again, I know that it's crazy.

A break between patients. Romain looks at his watch. For some time now a sledgehammer blow has been knocking him out around four o'clock. A pain grabs him by the nape of the neck. Fatigue overwhelms him until the last patient leaves, around six o'clock. If it were up to him he would cancel the rest of the day's appointments — imagine the look on Madame Beaurivage's face! He would go and pick up Thomas, take him downtown, show him street by street, house by house, the rebirth of the neighbourhood. They would hang out, talk about their childhood behaviour, good and bad. Without the father's presence between them they'd feel more comfortable. Thomas might even talk to him about the past five years.

Basically, thinks Romain, for five years now he and Thomas have had to submit to the same tyrant: medicine. Each in his own way. One on the side of the victors, the other the vanquished. Unless it's the other way around. Thomas had struck him as being so free, so peaceful, Romain hardly dares think of the word that would be most appropriate: happy. And what of him at this moment, with that iron bar across the nape of his neck, is he happy? Will the next patient, who in two minutes' time will be sitting across from him, tell him at once: "I am entrusting my body to a happy man"? Will he be reassured? Will Romain's happiness be powerful enough to knock out his own unhappiness? Patients expect so much of doctors.

Romain glances at the list. Ten more patients. Ten woes to strike down: worn-down bones, emphysema, alcohol-soaked livers, swollen glands. All, the same plea: to live! to live! All, the fear of non-existence. Despair. All, the demand for a miracle. Romain, the full list of the day's patients like so many needles planted in the nape of his neck. The longed-for miracle, he'll write the recipe on a page from a small pad with his name printed at the top of each one. Two tablets three times a day, one teaspoonful first thing in the morning and at bedtime. Trembling hands reach out for the paper. Eyes will thank him. Faith. Sickness is a furious dragon, thinks Romain, people believe that I've learned how to tame it. But I'm only its valet. Not a psychic either. Insupportable, those anxious faces that want to know when and how. As if the reply could slip easily out of his mouth: "Don't worry, Madame, you'll die gently, in your sleep, curled up in the warmth of your bed, you won't be aware of anything. I promise. And you, Monsieur, your death will be in the image of your life: horrible suffering will tear you to pieces. No medicine, no treatment will be able to ease it. I am truly sorry." When did death begin to be part of his life? A memory. Thomas, age eleven or twelve, runs up to him, steps over the fence that separates the two houses.

Under his arm, a big book bound in embossed fake leather. An encyclopedia. "I found something interesting!" Thomas's agitation. He reads slowly to Romain the page, which is not accompanied by an illustration. Funeral rites in India: bodies lying on a bed of flowers, the aroma of spices, the white of the fabric, the fire down to the minute heap of ashes. Thomas is deeply moved. Romain doesn't understand. Not yet. In the summer following this discovery, every fish, bird, toad found dead was entitled to a Hindu funeral on the shore. Stretcher made of branches, wildflowers, cremation amid the most absolute silence. Thomas, Brahman priest.

From the other side of the wall, Romain hears the muffled sound of the sewing machine. Life.

Madame Beaurivage knocks on the door.

"We're already running late this afternoon, Doctor."

"Yes, of course, send in the next patient," Romain replies, rubbing his neck.

T had chosen to step aside. From now on, time would belong to Joe, I would watch over the territory: a white house with its bit of beach and the body of a man. I thought that preparations for the move, the imminent prospect of leaving Chicago, would drive Joe crazy. Contrary to all expectations it put him in a good mood, he swam in the transitional universe of boxes and keep-this-get-rid-of-that like a fish in water. It didn't happen the way I'd expected. I was the one who had problems. Between fear of the unknown and the persistent fear of seeing Joe collapse in front of me, I put on a good act. I was no longer sure of anything, I couldn't sleep at night, all at once I didn't want to go away, a moment later I postponed the date of our departure, I had no appetite. I felt exhausted. But I went on with my act, superbly.

We've been living in the white house for two months now. We moved in at the beginning of August. When everything was unwrapped and put away, Joe surveyed the premises for a few days — now with the help of a cane — going from room to room, lingering on the terrace. With the suspicious manner of someone who doesn't believe what he sees. I kept expecting to hear: "It won't work, let's go, let's pack up and go back to Chicago." After two days he made just one brief remark, poorly enunciated, I could sense the effort behind the words: "It's great, baby, great!"

Without being really aware of it, we've organized the house like our Chicago apartment: an office for each of us, as far apart as possible, our common areas overloaded with travel photos and souvenirs. Joe has started playing the stock market online; he shows as much flair for it as for the import–export business. He spends an incredible amount of time with his eyes glued to his screen, looking at columns of figures. He has struck up a friendship with a retired neighbour; several times a week they get together to play chess. Stock market or chess, Joe's a gambler. Has the upper hand again.

Besides that, he has for the most part regained his motor skills. Like anyone who has come close to losing everything, he's hyperalert to simple pleasures, to the intensity of the moment. He's got used to his new life.

Unlike me.

I keep going around in circles. I don't know how to spend my time. I've said goodbye to my work as an illustrator, thinking that Joe would demand all my time. I have no more contracts. I've tried to carry on as if … I've drawn pretty well everything that grows between the house and the river. Even the seaweed washed up on shore at low tide. Sketches and watercolours pile up on my work table. Useless. Go out? Where? Definitely, Rimouski is not Chicago. And then the runaway syndrome has come back to haunt me: what if I met up with my mother or one of my brothers? I shut myself away in my office so Joe will think that all is well. I sit for hours watching the river and the sky. It's so big that I suffocate. I'm sixteen years old.

"I've got an idea!" Joe says one night when he comes home from his chess match. "We should get a dog. No, not *a* dog, two!"

Though we'd sworn that we'd never have children.

"Do you like dogs now?"

Seeing my lack of enthusiasm, Joe launches into a long, impassioned plea on the joy of living with dogs. Their infectious vitality, their unfailing loyalty. Water dogs, he makes clear, that goes without saying.

I don't object. I won't escape it. Joe wants a family life now. I just hope that I'll be better at it than my mother.

"*I* really have no choice," Romain tells Marie. "You could spend the afternoon with your parents. You know how they'd love to see the children ..."

"No choice! Do you think I do?" replies Marie, then immediately turns and walks away.

Romain's promise to Thomas's father against a Sunday in May with Marie and the children. He lied. Yes, he did have a choice. He could have kept his promise another time, could have asked Madame Beaurivage not to make any appointments after five o'clock on such and such a day. He could have gone to see Thomas, talked to him, then come home for supper and for Marie's smile. What has actually happened is that all week Thomas's face hasn't left him. It is with Thomas that he'd like to spend the afternoon. He must talk to him of course, it's urgent, but as far as he knows, nothing prevents an emergency from being a pretext too. Just this once. It won't kill Marie.

There's no question of her paying a Sunday visit to the parents. Before what time is it indecent to hit the Scotch? she wonders.

Thomas was waiting for a sign. He was happy when Romain phoned to suggest a guided tour of downtown. Not because of the visit — he'd done that again and again with Rex, nearly every day since his arrival — but for Romain himself. Thomas's memory was hard at work, but Romain was resisting him. By setting foot in this town, Thomas had rediscovered odours, places, voices — a whole world, in short, which he had reconstituted from a distance over the years at the cost of daily exhausting efforts. But Romain refused to return to his niche in Thomas's brain. Thomas and his memory were in agreement: he had to attack. Take by force this man who insisted on their shared childhood and shove him away some-where, anywhere, in his head.

Thomas didn't want Romain to call for him at his parents' place. He would rather go to Romain's. "I'll see where you live," he said to explain his refusal. Which is not the real reason. If Romain had come to get him Thomas wouldn't have dared impose on him the presence of Rex in his car. With this arrangement Romain will find himself before a *fait accompli*.

Early afternoon. Marie hasn't left. Romain is waiting impatiently for Thomas, who is walking with his dog towards the house of a stranger who is also his best friend from childhood.

If old Doctor Rhéaume's house — no one in town has rechristened it with Romain's name since the young couple moved in there — is so imposing from the outside, the land it stands on impresses Thomas even more as he studies it with a gardener's eyes.

An enormous property lined with big maples and, here and there between the trees, the remains of what must have been a hedge. The house, a big blot of red brick, strangely off-centre, stands at the end of it, an ornate iron fence, low, surrounds it and separates it from the possibility of a botanical garden. In any case, that is what Thomas tells himself, hands on hips, in front of the big green rectangle, where the only vegetation is a blemished lawn. In his eyes, a sacrilege. He already sees beds of roses, shrubs, islands of rare plants next to which benches would be placed. All of it strategically laid out with attention paid to the amount of sunlight and the first sight of it from the street.

The first time, the first impression. So here he is, the thief of Sunday, planted in the middle of the property with a dog at his feet. Here is this Thomas whom Romain has been talking about all week. He raises his head, studies the trees, then looks at the ground, to the left, to the right. Without leaving the kitchen window, Marie says to Romain, over the children's babbling: "Your friend is waiting outside. I think he's afraid to knock on the door." Romain rushes past Marie, who hands him his jacket, oh, the murderous look in her eyes.

They're already a trio, they don't know it. Marie at her post sees Romain extend his hand to the hand of this stranger and clasp it. Their smiles. Romain grinning from ear to ear,

Thomas's smile more discreet. The two men strike up a conversation. The dog sniffs Romain's legs. With slow and measured movements, Thomas points to certain maple trees; Romain's, broad and quick, answer him. After a moment, they head for the house. "Shit!" says Marie, who won't escape the official introduction.

Abruptly, Marie takes the baby out of the playpen and holds him close. Her shield. The other two, surprised at their mother's movement, come and cling to her. Don't move now, the portrait is perfect for launching Romain's guilt.

Thomas doesn't budge from the door, he's intimidated. First by Marie's perceptible hostility. No smile, a reluctant, brittle *bonjour*. Intimidated too by the youngsters frozen in front of him.

"Let me introduce my wife, Marie, and my three sons."

The number seems enormous.

"Three, already?" he lets slip. "That's quite a family!"

Then, realizing that he might have offended them, he adds: "Congratulations!"

Thomas's reaction didn't fall on deaf ears, and Marie suddenly decides that there's something almost likable about this tall, skinny man whose left shoulder is higher than the other. What she would like most at this very moment is for the three children to perform their choral work — another of Romain's expressions — that is, to start bawling and howling in chorus, something to give the imminent departure of Romain and Thomas the sense of a Greek tragedy. But for once they're silent, all three clinging to their mother.

Romain, his hand on the doorknob. If he could jump, he would, thinks Marie.

"Aren't you coming with us?" Thomas asks with disarming sincerity, as if it went without saying.

The question delights Marie. Definitely, this tall, skinny type is a nice guy.

"As you say, three children is quite a family — to haul around. Especially on a beautiful Sunday in spring."

Romain turns the doorknob, Marie smiles faintly to thank Thomas. What he retains from the young woman's eyes is neither her frustration nor her disagreement nor the promise of love, only her distress. And not just any distress, but the worst kind of all, the kind he knows best: distress related to a hospital.

Already Marie and Thomas are a length ahead of Romain. After all, trios are triangles, of which the angles are not necessarily equal.

From the red night, a new world has been born. A dot, a tiny cell on the planet, a neighbourhood turned resolutely towards modernity. At once an object of pride and of pity. Undeniable proof, five years later, of victory over adversity. Romain is playing tourist guide. The date, the day, and the hour, what the weather is like, the damn wires and poles, the electric lightning in the Price Company lumberyard. The fire, the sirens, the river thought to be impossible to cross.

The wild wind that had started carrying incandescent comets. The house, the incredulity, the fear. The conflagration, the apocalypse. Not one detail missing. As if it were yesterday.

"What were you doing then, Romain?"

"I was in my room in Quebec City, packing my bags!"

"And your wife?"

"She was helping the nuns in the convent who were taking in people who'd come there for refuge."

And so, thinks Thomas, in case of emergency Marie's memory will be better able to fraternize with mine. Romain's is useless: it's a prefabricated memory that knows everything that needs to be known. But all that, it has learned from the outside. It has been imposed to such a degree that it recounts how events unfolded while saying: "We thought … We didn't assess the situation properly … We reacted …" A memory that borders on imposture, the worst crime, in Thomas's book.

What Romain has been talking about for practically an hour doesn't interest Thomas. He thinks he's listening to the newspaper articles he was told to read in the hospital. Of which he takes advantage: could there be in Romain's movements, in the inflection of his voice, in the confidence of his gaze, a small flaw, a minute crack through which to reach the childhood road on which Thomas could set out with Romain so that his friend could resume the place that he's demanding loud and clear? That's what Thomas is tracking down unbeknownst to Romain.

Once the neighbourhood has been surveyed and the disaster

classified as over and done with, Thomas suggests they walk along the river. Romain moves on to phase two of his plan. The promise made to the father. Something gives him away — his voice perhaps, his movements, his gaze — all have become more hesitant. Thomas understands that the afternoon will not be summed up merely as blocks of houses that have been rebuilt.

Romain, his introduction. Every sentence begins, "Remember when …" Games, bonfires on the beach, dead eels left on the doorstep of a loathsome neighbour. Thomas listens without flinching, asks some questions to make Romain expand on his remarks. Later, when he's alone, he will try to find something. For now, Romain is someone he still doesn't know, and what he tells, a charred zone in his memory. Finally, Romain is silent for a moment. To catch his breath. They're now on the shore, the afternoon is advancing, the tide is at its highest. Thomas skips stones across the water.

"I haven't shut up. Your turn! How's your homecoming?" asks Romain.

Who is actually speaking? Thomas wonders. The friend? The physician? His parents' aide-de-camp? What can he say in reply to this strange man who has been asking questions since the beginning of the afternoon, then answering them at once with a confidence that he'll never have? Romain wants to know how things are going. Very well. Both for him and for the town. A transformation of which it is hard to say whether it's more attractive or uglier than before. New houses without a soul, some built on the foundations of old ones. Empty spaces too that are yet to be filled in. Determination and fragility that are united though.

"It's all right."

Thomas says nothing more.

"It can't be easy, coming back after all this time, you and your parents haven't seen each other since …"

Thomas realizes suddenly that Romain is on a mission, that it is from him that one of the keys he has come here in search of will come.

"Do you want to talk? Go ahead, just remember, I'm not very good at detours."

"You haven't changed! You've always been direct! Yes, it's true, your father doesn't know how to go about it, he's asked me to talk to you because he figures that it's easier between friends than between a father and son."

"Out with it!"

"Well, you see … basically … no one here ever knew that you'd gone to Quebec City."

"Interned would be more accurate," Thomas points out.

"As you wish. Your parents said that you'd run away, that you'd left a letter to explain. During all these years they've been putting on an act. Grief-stricken parents, vaguely concerned, then time passes, the questions stopped. It was easier for them …"

"… than admitting that their son was in the asylum," Thomas continued. "It's all right, I suspected it. I've had five years to understand the disgrace, the embarrassment, the shame. I've seen parents, brothers, sisters hug the walls in the hospital corridors. I've seen them look up at the clock every two minutes, I've seen them eager to leave the minute they arrive. But I interrupted you, finish your sermon, here, I'll help you: I saw lots of people but I didn't see my parents, I'm sure you have an explanation for that too."

In Thomas's voice, for the first time, some disgust.

"Don't shoot the messenger. Yes, you're right, I'm doing your parents' errands, but that doesn't mean I approve of their behaviour. You explained it yourself: some people, apparently, can't overcome shame."

"You've come in their name to negotiate the rest? Tell them not to worry, there isn't much in me that pills and treatments haven't got under control. There won't be a crisis, no scandal, no red night. Or, no, don't tell them anything! If they haven't understood yet that I didn't come back for them, it's not worth the trouble."

"So who did you come back for?"

"Myself, just for myself."

Romain would like to know the story from the inside, from Thomas's mouth. Would like to rub out the parents' version, which he listened to patiently, taking notes now and then, not letting it show how upset he was. Go back to the beginning, to the precise moment when the gears in Thomas's brain jammed, follow him during the slow descent of the body that didn't anticipate the danger, has let itself glide, docile, and then at the end see him hit the walls, at once howling and silent, let himself be inundated by the unbelievable suffering, collapse under its weight, become deaf to the voices that were trying to help him up. See him listening only to the character inside him. The one who wanted to kill him.

Thomas is aware of Romain's goodwill, but beyond the role of mediator that he plays as best he can, there is someone who escapes him. Because of the gap in his memory. The loyalty to what they once were for one another, the transparency, Thomas gets from Romain, undeniably. His sincerity is touching. The attention Romain pays shakes him, even if he doesn't let it show. Till now, no one has asked him to describe it. Neither the descent into hell, nor the hell, nor the loneliness after the hell. But he won't talk. One can't describe things like that. Not to a stranger anyway. If his memory restores Romain to him, yes, maybe. If he becomes again the boy with skinned knees howling with laughter at their latest rotten trick, if he really is the person he's been claiming to be since Thomas's return.

Romain doesn't push it. They haven't said anything for several minutes. They are sitting on rocks. The tide is ebbing, the river receding. Rex's head on Thomas's knees. Petting him. No longer alone. The afternoon is ending. The grey-green of the river. Marie's eyes. Her afternoon. Her gaze, which Romain has avoided. Her gaze given to Thomas.

*F*or thirty years, I've kept a photo in a sealed envelope inside a box made of lacquered wood. My sole relic from the past. When I was leaving, at the very last moment, when I was on the doorstep, I turned around; I ran to the living room, which we never used, I took the photo out of its ornamental gold frame. I was trembling. The frame slipped out of my hands, the glass shattered into a thousand pieces on the floor. I was afraid the noise would wake up my brothers. I left it there on the varnished floor, in front of the fireplace, ineluctable proof that I'd run away. I've never looked at that photo again, I swear. Joe doesn't even know that it exists.

I don't know what's got into me this morning — no doubt the business of the dogs that Joe has been harping on about for days now — all I can think about is that photo. I'm alone. Joe has just left with the neighbour: visit to the local kennels.

The way is clear.

Though I've never looked at it, I have always arranged things so that it's not too far away. A true ceremony: the box open in front of me, the envelope, my hand slowly slipping inside, taking it.

The colours are unchanged. We are frozen in a pose for all eternity. Around us, like a rampart, the garden. Flowers, beds, trees, the beautiful summer light. All of us.

I must be a little more than a year old. I'm wearing the regulation uniform for little girls at the time — a pale pink dress with puffed sleeves and smocking. In my hair, a ribbon bow in the same colour as the dress. I am the only one who's not smiling; I even look worried, obviously not understanding what's going on in front of me. I'm sitting on Yvonne's lap. From the way she is embracing me one can sense her fondness for me. At the time she still wore her hair in a chignon, I only ever knew her with grey hair. Yvonne has always been old. I adored her. The back of the wicker chair we're sitting in has a hole in one spot. It could have used a coat of paint too. Surprising when you know my mother and her obsession with appearances. On the left in the photo, my mother is also sitting in a wicker chair. She sits very straight. Dignified, regal despite her frozen smile, her absent gaze. Standing close to her, André, the youngest of my brothers, clutching her legs, snot-nosed and dressed in his Sunday best. Obviously the most important thing that's happening in this photo is at the centre, between the wicker chairs. My father, squatting with one knee on the ground and one of my other two brothers on either side. All three are chuckling. In front of them, eyes fixed on the camera, his gaze even more absent than my mother's, is Rex, the only dog we ever had, and if it weren't for the photos and the way my father worshipped him, talked about him incessantly, I wouldn't remember the animal who died two or three years after I was born. It's funny; in my memory Rex was a huge dog. In the photos we have he was always posed with my brothers, at the time very young, which granted him a stature that he lost automatically in the presence of adults, as here for instance, where my squatting father looks like a giant. In my mind too Rex was a purebred; instead, I am looking at an old mutt of indefinite colour, with medium-length hair. In our family legend, Rex held an important place. A kind of mythic character that my father referred to often as a model when he claimed that we weren't brave enough. I don't recall exactly what he said, but roughly, it was that Rex had had a hard life, he'd been mistreated, he'd lost his master, found him, then lost him again. To say nothing of the fact that he was blind and deaf.

A perfect symmetry emanates from the portrait. The wicker chair at either end: the world of women and babies. In the middle, the world of men: my father, his sons, harmoniously — or hierarchically — placed. And in the front row, Rex, the warm heart of this little tribe.

A family. Noise. Movement. Shouts.

I won't put the photo back in its box. I feel ridiculous. As if the fact of waiting thirty years before opening the envelope revealed in me an exceptional gift for endurance. While I didn't resist, I wasn't tempted to open it until today. What's most pitiful is that I'd thought it took only a sealed envelope in a box at the back of a closet to wipe out a section of life. To erase childhood.

The photo will join another — which shows me naked, from the back, advancing into the Caribbean — between the pages of my big atlas of South America.

Oh, the look on Joe's face when he came home at the end of the day! The neighbour set down a cage. From it came, frightened, two blond balls — golden retrievers, a male and a female. After a few moment's hesitation, they began to inspect the premises, timidly, with much sniffing. After that they started running around in every direction. I don't remember ever seeing Joe with that look on his face, like an ecstatic little boy. I always thought that of the two of us, I was the child, that Joe was still clinging to the image of a little girl lost in Toronto's bus terminal. It was a convenient impression: it stopped me from aging. The two dogs in my house have just made me thirty years older in one go.

*I*n the hospital, every night at bedtime Thomas was overtaken by anxiety. Of all the forms that tyrannized him, that one particular anxiety was the most loathsome in his eyes, though it had never aspired to the intensity of some other forms. Thomas was intensely irritated by it: he called it his bogeyman, the anxiety of a little boy whose mother was far away. It had appeared around the end of his stay, at the moment when his discharge was beginning to break through on the horizon and the quantity of pills he had to swallow every day was diminishing. A nurse who was quite fond of Thomas sensed it. She sometimes sat on the edge of his bed; she was still young despite her grey hair. She was eagle-eyed. Thomas was fond of her too. With her, never any fuss. She had simply told him to let himself go and dream, that it worked better than sleeping pills. That sleep would come quickly, as if by magic, attracted by his dream, and then they would be one. The night would be pleasant. Thomas had retorted that it would be hard to dream when he was missing large chunks of memory. "Wrong, Thomas," she had replied, "you're confusing dreams and memories. Dreams are ahead of you."

Thomas had got down to work. He applied himself but he wasn't getting there. Neither dreams nor memories wanted him. He could not imagine himself in any reality. Nowhere did he feel at ease. Not in the arms of a woman who took on the features and the body of the young girl who'd just arrived upstairs, and who, every time someone approached her, banged her head violently against the wall. Her beauty was still dazzling despite her collapse. Nor in a triumphant image of himself. When he saw himself free, well-dressed, laughing in the midst of people who liked to think of themselves as familiar, his dream came close to nightmare. But he did not necessarily reject the technique. He needed that small victory. To avenge all those he hadn't had since arriving at the hospital, all those of which the prospect had not stirred in him the taste of battle. Resolutely, though, he'd finally got there. He had developed a strategy. The trick was to choose a subject and stick to it. He'd understood that when he was excluded from the scenario, the idea seemed to want to settle in, letting the anxiety die away by itself. The more interesting the idea, the less hold anxiety had. You needed a simple subject — not a problem to solve — a subject that would not develop, that would have neither ins nor outs. A subject that would unfurl in the moment. In April then his subject became seasonal when Thomas was working in the hospital's greenhouses. Before falling asleep he repeated the movements he'd accomplished during the day. But it was no longer tomato seedlings that had to be transplanted into small wooden boxes that mattered, it was the infinite gentleness he must put into the act of separating the tangled plants; minuscule, fragile, still attached to the seeds that they had been. And now the seeds that had germinated, driven by an uncontrolled energy, were trying to wipe out the neighbour that was threatening the living space. Patient fingers handled them and repeated in the language of fingers that there would be a place for each of them. That infinite gentleness combined with the rough perfume of the young plants did more for Thomas than a tranquilizer.

So he had put together a collection of scenarios, all linked to the seasons and to horticulture. Ritual became instinct and started up as soon as Thomas switched off the lamp. It had continued after he left the hospital, even though the anxiety was no longer present at the rendezvous.

Once the lamps were out, all the rooms resembled each other. Whether in a psychiatric hospital, a modest building in a workers' neighbourhood, or the basement of a house in Rimouski. Darkness, night have no fine distinctions. Here in this cellar there's no need for ritual. Rex has taken over. Thomas just has to listen. Is it the lamp that he switches off — does Rex experience light? — that gives the dog the signal? Or the hand that strokes his neck just before the big lean body that he follows like a shadow topples and stretches out full-length on the bed? Or the air displaced by the covers that are folded down with a snap and that separate him from Thomas until morning? Rex then undertakes a final round. He has traced a path for himself, a visit to the cellar, over which he has control now, after Thomas has shifted all the objects the dog has bumped his head on. Rex takes his time, sniffs the same odours night after night, lingers at the same spots. His paws scraping on the cement floor. He watches over Thomas. If Rex could talk, he would say: it's all right, you can sleep, I've checked everything. No ghosts, no demons, no sparks to set fire to the town. Then Rex goes back to his home base, flattens the quilted tartan bedspread as if he were replacing a layer of imaginary straw, and flops onto it, curled up in a ball. Six seconds later — Thomas has timed it — Rex heaves a great sigh, then sinks into sleep.

In the hospital, there was a high-security wing. Access to it was impossible. Thomas hadn't understood at first what the designation signified. He imagined that it must be the site of supreme happiness: high security. Wasn't that what all sick people look for, desperately? Only a few left their wing for the high-security one. Thomas wondered why he hadn't been sent there. The eagle-eyed nurse had explained to him that the expression "high security" didn't exactly mean heaven on Earth. Thomas had been ashamed of his naïveté, but had held onto the expression in his personal lexicon. At the time, nothing else summed up so well what he expected of life. Now, every evening Rex offered him five minutes of high security.

At night sometimes Thomas wakes up. Certain questions become urgent. He tries to modulate his answers to the rhythm of Rex's breathing. It is now several weeks that he's been back, summer is at the gates. In Quebec City, on the Plains of Abraham, the gardeners must be busy transplanting annuals. The task that Thomas likes best. A happy frenzy settles into the crew. A kind of blitz, you have to move fast even if there's no rush. The planting is done very early in the morning or late in the afternoon. For Thomas, the world cannot be more orderly than it is during this task: here, the marigolds, now yellow, now orange; there, petunias. Such is life in the sun: in rows, in squares, in circles, or triangles.

In Rimouski though, there's no Plains of Abraham, no gardener. Only the blue that swallows everything. Here, beauty is liquid. Given that, Thomas thinks as he listens to Rex's breathing, maybe it would be better to go back to Quebec City? He's a little annoyed with himself. He hadn't foreseen everything. The thought of coming back had imposed itself abruptly. He had followed his instinct. Left his room, his work, packed his bags. He had a little money. He won't find work — he only knows how to be a gardener — his scant savings are used up. He sleeps in a cellar. In the house of his parents, who obviously can't relax in his company.

He had been propelled there by a sensation, an impression that he was going to start again. What was lacking would be given to him. It could be called hope. Or his due. He doesn't see himself pacing the banks of the river or the streets of town with Rex all summer long. Even his memory lapses have lost interest. In the end, rediscovering childhood with Romain is unimportant. Romain exists in the present, that's enough, he expects nothing more. Rediscovering a child-hood friend has no more weight than making a new one.

And yet he is waiting for something. Here as in Quebec City. When his hands were buried in the ground, waiting was manageable. But summer is here and his hands are clean, he misses having earth under his nails. All the time.

Anxiety is back, when he wakes up in the middle of the night. Rex's discreet snoring doesn't stand in his way. The question Romain had asked the first time they saw each other, when they were walking on the shore, pounded at his head: "What do you think you'll do here?"

Thomas, who hadn't known what to reply, had felt ashamed. An incompetent gardener.

And in the darkness of the cellar, to curb the progress of the distress that fills his chest, that is speeding up his breathing, Thomas works. He digs up big clumps of peat moss, turns over the earth that he has just freed, spades it, breaks it up, works hard to pull out the roots. His movements have lost their usual slowness. He is filled with a kind of fever. The strength, the vigour he puts into the task are unlike him. Thomas dreams in order to summon sleep: he transforms Romain's big, neglected property into a garden.

$\mathcal{M}$y brothers and I lived in separate universes. I wasn't admitted into theirs. I was the one who'd come after. After what? I was never able to say. The age difference wasn't that great — less than two years between me and the youngest. For a long time I thought it was because I was a girl. Because of a lack of affinities we didn't share much, neither games nor pastimes. My brothers were restless and noisy. I was quiet and silent. I drew — it seems to me that I knew no other activity — sitting at a small table Yvonne had set up for me next to her in my mother's sewing room — where I'd never seen her sew a stitch, by the way.

My parents ruled over their four subjects. Each in his own way. My father was a good man. Unquestionably taken up by his work, and a sports enthusiast — an enthusiasm he shared with his sons. The occupations of the queen mother varied according to the season and her mood. In the winter, she read, played bridge with her circle of women friends, smoked, and drank a Scotch every evening before supper while watching television, a sacred moment, kindly do not disturb. Summers she spent in the garden. She never raised her voice against us. She saw to it that we lacked nothing. Life seemed to run off her back like water off a duck's.

I wasn't sidelined. On the contrary, I was the family mascot. A little clown, a cute little doll. Yes, that's the right word — a mascot. Like those big plush animals that cheer on the team and that the fans love.

The mascot belongs to the team. Isn't part of it.

I always wondered if the mascots shared the players' room or if they had their own. They probably have a personal locker room. A mascot who undresses in front of the players, suspending a costume on a huge hanger, careful not to flatten the fluffy fabric, taking off the big clown head while the players, eager to be on their way, look on absent-mindedly, is impossible, unthinkable. When she takes off her skin, she has no choice but to be alone. A mascot never appears naked in front of the family.

My brothers though knew how to use the mascot. For instance, a few years after Rex died, they wanted another dog. Their wish went unheeded. They took it up again regularly, and every time they got a categorical refusal from my mother. Though they tried their luck with my father, he put up a united front with his wife. My brothers, who did know something about my father's interest in dogs, had orchestrated one final attempt when my mother was in the hospital. They'd put me in charge of the mission. Taking advantage of my mother's absence, I was the one, at age six, who was supposed to make my father give in. My brothers instructed me: I had to move him, repeat the request every day while stepping up the quaver in my voice, and, ideally, if I could shed a few tears it would be in the bag. After one week I'd become a specialist in grovelling harassment. My brothers encouraged me, they were unusually kind. In my daily briefings I lied. I told them I was on the brink of success, though actually my father was adamant. In fact I think that after my second plea he actually stopped listening. And so I failed miserably. My brothers were furious. The youngest bit me, the others scratched me. Worse than dogs.

The memory is bitter. It masked what was important: my mother wasn't there and life was going on. With its little nasty remarks, its affection in the eyes of Yvonne, its glorious light in the garden.

I didn't know why my mother was in the hospital. "Don't worry, sweetheart, your mama will be home soon, the doctors are going to fix her up really, really fast," Yvonne repeated tirelessly when I asked her why Mama was in the hospital.

It was not till later, five or six years later, when she fell into another depression, that I knew.

⁓

THE LAST TWO PATIENTS of the day are chatting quietly when Thomas comes into the waiting room. They barely look in his direction. On the telephone, Madame Beaurivage is passing on figures and data to another person who keeps asking her to repeat what she's just said. Thomas sits down and stretches his legs out in front of him.

Madame Beaurivage, who has just hung up, regards him from the corner of her eye.

"Do you have an appointment, sir?"

"No."

"Doctor Lemieux only sees patients by appointment. Except for emergencies," she adds, thinking that this boy who is practically slumped in his chair doesn't look too unwell.

"I'll wait," replies Thomas with a hint of a smile.

"That's not the point," she goes on. "Everyone's day has to come to an end."

"I'm not here to consult the doctor. I'm a friend of Romain's."

There is a pregnant pause. The patients stop talking: he has referred to the doctor by his first name. Madame Beaurivage wonders if she should believe him. She knows everything about Romain's life. He doesn't have time to have friends. He barely has enough for Marie and the children.

"Fine, in that case you can see him after his patients," she says. "I'll tell him you're here. You are Monsieur ..."

"Thomas."

And because one cannot exist with just a first name, he adds: "Garant. Thomas Garant."

In Madame Beaurivage's eyes, a spark.

With no fuss, Thomas has just emerged from anonymity. His father's disgrace suddenly descends on him.

Right away, Romain is excited. The plan suggested by Thomas, which he backs up with slow, precise gestures — he has already drawn up everything — presents only advantages. Thomas would be there every day; he would do his gardening work while Romain was doing his right next door. Patience and indulgence. We would be together, thinks Romain, the timing couldn't be better. Romain is well aware of Thomas's urgent need for dignity; he is definitely not asking for charity. Marie could take part in the choice of plants, she would certainly like the idea of a garden, women like flowers, everyone knows how much women like flowers. Romain even sees himself on Sunday giving Thomas a hand with the heavy work. Nearby, Marie and the boys. A smiling Marie.

It's a deal, Thomas, your dignity against a breath of fresh air in my realm. We'll be even. That's the message from Romain's hand on Thomas's shoulder.

Madame Beaurivage, who usually finishes her workday when the last patient goes into Romain's office, has found some dossiers to file. He can't be a friend. Five years ago that boy was stark raving mad. Then disappeared mysteriously. Dead, without a doubt. His parents claimed that he'd gone away, leaving a letter for them. She had always believed that they'd clung to that supposition because it was less frightening than the other. In any event, deranged as he was, he wouldn't have survived anywhere else.

Thomas and Romain leave the office, laughing. Thomas has accepted Romain's invitation to dinner.

"You're still here, Madame Beaurivage? Did you two have a chance to get acquainted?" Romain asks, with a questioning look at both Thomas and Madame Beaurivage. Without giving them time to reply, he goes on: "Thomas will be spending the summer with us, there's going to be action around here!" He reveals nothing more and leads Thomas towards the big polished oak door, leaving Madame Beaurivage's curiosity unsatisfied.

Romain takes up all the space. He's inexhaustible. Thomas only speaks when Romain asks something specific about the project. Marie listens to them, fiddling vaguely with the fork on her plate.

"It's going to be wonderful! Are you happy?" Romain asks her.

"Yes, of course," she replies tersely.

If it weren't for Thomas's presence, she would reply that it confirms what she already thinks: the entire universe has plans, anyone in this town, doctor or nutcase, knows when he gets up in the morning that he won't be spending the day changing diapers. Sure, she likes flowers — who doesn't? — they smell so lovely, they're so beautiful to look at — if you have the time.

Neither animosity nor enthusiasm. "Go outside and play,

boys," she would like to tell Romain and Thomas — a remark that she has never uttered and that she'll repeat ad nauseam over the next twelve years — "Leave mama alone, she has dishes, sewing, cleaning, cooking, reading to finish." The choice will be unlimited.

Romain feels that once again, he's missed the target. He wishes he could make her happy. After all, it's not a bed of dandelions they're being offered.

Thomas looks at Marie. She is standing at the same distance as she had the first time they met. A shiver up his spine: nothing is stronger than the appeal of a person whose appeal is silent.

After Thomas leaves, Marie questions Romain. Will he be there every day? Is he normal? Reliable? Isn't there a danger that the plan might fizzle out? He can't turn dangerous, can he? Or his dog? The two eldest are starting to play outside ...

"Marie, come on, you've seen him just as I have, is there anything about him that doesn't seem right?"

Marie can say nothing in reply.

"He's all right, you see, don't worry. Anyway, you won't have to be with him. I trust him, you mustn't think I'm doing him a favour. In fact I'm repaying a debt. I'm not sure that what he went through over the past five years, even if he hasn't really talked to me about it, would give medicine anything to be proud of."

"So the worthy physician is starting to doubt his knowledge? That's new, I've never seen you like this."

"It happens, Marie, it happens. More often than I'd like."

Two days later, in the early evening shortly after the boys' bath, Thomas comes back. He has bought equipment: hoses, shovels, a rake, a fork, planters. Romain goes out to give him a hand. The garage at the end of the driveway will be Thomas's headquarters. The older boy, who has climbed up on a stool, is at the kitchen window, eager for action. He wants to go outside with his papa and the man, wants to play with the dog, wants to drive the red truck in front of the garage. Marie is looking at them too. From now on each of them will have a particular reason for looking outside.

From a great, silent temple, the house has now become a kind of tower of Babel. Two puppies are equivalent to at least four children. We've even clashed, Joe and I, on the question of their education. He wanted to bring them up in English, I in French. I served him arguments straight out of the seventies; I also mentioned that we'd look like idiots in public places, on the street, with our commands: Sit! Stop! Down! Heel!

"Are we going to go for walks?" he replied, at once caustic and mocking, but even more, with the slightly painful expression that marks his efforts now when he speaks.

He's right. We aren't going anywhere. Genuine loners.

We finally agreed on a half-and-half lexicon. Training dogs is serious work! It takes up a lot of time, Joe's in particular. I allowed myself to get caught up in the game. I didn't think I'd get attached to them so quickly. But I'm not fooled. Their presence fills a void, makes up for something that I can't define, either to myself or to Joe. If I can't do it, it's because the question is multiple choice: Joe's physical condition? The bustling activity of Chicago? The handsome cowboy and the little hippie girl have aged and no other character has replaced them? Their life on the bank of the river is boring? Which reply is correct? None of the above? All?

All of the above.

Go out. We should go out. I'm going to take Joe to a restaurant on his birthday. If we never go out, it's because of him. When his motor functions became acceptable again, when he progressed from a walker to a cane, I thought to myself that finally the period of house arrest was over. But no, Joe doesn't like to exhibit the proof of his body's decomposition, as he puts it. He's exaggerating, I remind him over and over. He limps, he walks slowly, so what? Pride is a deadly sin that will lead him to hell. He doesn't believe me. O man of little faith.

Except to me and the neighbour, he doesn't like to talk either. His problems with aphasia have for the most part faded, but there are after-effects. In the presence of someone with whom he's not familiar, Joe often has to repeat himself. The situation gets complicated when he speaks French with his heavy accent.

For tonight though he hasn't been able to say no to me. I'd already invited the neighbour and his wife. Joe tried to persuade me to entertain them at home instead of in a restaurant. A waste of time, we go out.

It's been ages since we've dressed up. Joe is a good-looking man. He wasn't when I first met him; he was a little later, around forty. He became incredibly charming at the time his first wrinkles appeared.

Elegant restaurant perched in an old manor house, gourmet cuisine. Joe can't get over it: of course we left behind civilization and its refinements when we moved to this remote land. The atmosphere is festive. Our neighbour, Jean, and his wife, Hélène, are delightful. They're the same age as Joe. They celebrated their wedding anniversary a few weeks ago. I will have spent my life with people older than me.

Alcohol flows freely. Drinking makes our companions cheerful. Joe is having fun. I don't feel like drinking.

*F*or a while now Marie has been feeling a kind of disgust. She can't understand why. At first it was just an external image, which concerned not her but Romain. It had cropped up suddenly in the sewing room one afternoon. The children were asleep, she was sitting at the sewing machine, and her feet refused to work it. Silence prevailed in the house so intensely that Marie seemed transfixed. She just had to close her eyes and her head turned into a wash basin: everything she consisted of at this precise moment — her body, her rage, her maternal impulses, her irrepressible need to end up on a desert island — was going down the drain. What remained was the smooth, white, shiny inner surfaces. Then, on the other side of the wall, Romain had shown in his first patient of the afternoon. The usual murmur had brought Marie back to life. She then did something that she'd never allowed herself to do: listen in. Nothing had filtered through, but all at once the wall that separated her from Romain had become transparent. She hadn't seen him as she'd always liked to picture him: sitting impassively at his desk, the mahogany furniture conferring on him the authority and the distance he was required to maintain with his patients. No, she had seen him in the examining room, bending over a body that lay there, abandoned and vulnerable.

All day long Romain's hands palpate bodies. Bodies of children and teenage boys, of young girls and pregnant women. Bodies that give one an urge to slowly glide one's hands so that the gesture becomes a caress. Skin filled with future, firm or plump, pink, tender skins, sometimes streaked with veins, small blue paths, mysterious, holding secrets of which they reveal only the colour. But above all there are the others. Bodies whose odours, as soon as the office door is shut, catch at your throat. Drab clothes cover them. Then they strip. Squalor, decay, or old age. Bruised, mutilated, exhausted bodies. Romain's hands on those bodies. His fingers — the rubber gloves make no difference — in stinking anuses, his fingers lancing abscesses full of pus. Blood, mucus, bacteria, viruses. To say nothing of foul-smelling breath, grime, scabs. Romain's hands all day long burrowed in chaos.

Romain's hands on her body. On her mouth, her sex. Romain's hands on his children's sacred flesh.

Marie gagged. Ran to the toilet, sure she was going to vomit.

Since that afternoon Marie has kept an eye on Romain's hands. They're always impeccable. Which isn't enough. Obsessive, the images of sick bodies don't let go. Romain's hands touch everyone. Marie thinks about it every time he puts his hands on her or on the boys. There's no rational explanation.

Marie, in bed, leafs through a magazine. Romain is with Thomas, helping him remove equipment from the truck.

The two men are taking their time. The evening is mild. Romain got it into his head that eventually he would make Thomas talk, wear him down. Thomas talked, yes, Romain learned step by step the horticultural program for the week to come. It's a start, he thought.

"He seems to know what he's doing," he tells Marie as he goes into the bedroom.

"That's good," she replies vaguely, without taking her nose out of her magazine.

It's an evening of firsts. The first time that Thomas is between them. Marie has switched off the lamp, Romain goes on talking for a long moment. Romain's interest in Thomas is surprising, she thinks. First time too that Marie shrinks away when Romain lays his hands on her belly. All the images of sick bodies that have been flooding her for some time are now all jumbled together. Impossible to flee those images, or Romain's warm white hands. Marie dissolves into tears. Head buried in the pillow so her sobs won't be transformed into a scream. Romain strokes her hair. When a few minutes later Marie calms down a little, between two bouts of tears he murmurs in her ear: "Starting tomorrow, Yvonne is going to come every day."

Marie does not resist. Fatigue is a more common feeling than disgust.

Yvonne enters Marie's life through the polished oak door. She will follow to the letter the instructions of the doctor, who told her to stop by his office before going to the house.

Starting now, the days will be lighter, the boys won't squall so much. Summer will spread its warmth over Marie. Suddenly, there will be time. Yvonne's time against Marie's. The fatigue of the one on the shoulders of the other.

He arrives so early in the morning. Sometimes before she goes down to the kitchen with the boys. While Romain is still asleep and Yvonne goes to Mass before coming to preside over the destiny of the tribe. Marie observes him. Already he is bustling about at his work. Like her. As if they were the first man and the first woman in this town to be taken up by the day. Thomas follows rigorously the plan he suggested to them. At the moment, he is preparing wide bands of loose soil at the limits of the property. Gradually he'll move closer to the house. Before she goes inside to work, Yvonne always chats with him. Sometimes she takes a package from her big bag: cookies, cakes, even bones for Rex. She pets the dog's head. Then heads for the house, whistling to herself. Every morning, when Yvonne steps into the kitchen, Marie feels a pang that resembles jealousy. Years later, Marie will tell herself that was how it all started. With that small daily dose of irritation: Thomas's smile offered to Yvonne and not to her.

When it rains, Thomas doesn't come. The almanac forecasts a perfect summer: sunny days, rain only at night. Yvonne swears by these predictions. Marie catches herself hoping that they're true.

From the window in the kitchen or the sewing room, Marie looks at Thomas. Simply a game, an illusion, a distraction.

Some weeks pass, Thomas and Marie don't run into each other. In the afternoon, after the boys' nap, Marie settles in with them close to the house. The older ones play with trucks; Marie has put the baby on a blanket. Thomas waves broadly to them. He doesn't stop, never comes over to see them.

After work, Romain no longer goes through the big oak door systematically like before, he joins Thomas, who shows him what he has accomplished that day. Romain brings the bottle of Scotch to the garage. That's how the day ends now. In the sun, outside the garage, sitting on overturned wooden crates, the one describing the life cycle of a plant, which he calls by its Latin name, the other despairing over the life cycle of a patient he doesn't name. It's the hour of forgiveness, when the light transforms men's fatigue into the mirage of an oasis.

In the house, meanwhile, it's time for reheating. Yvonne has just gone, leaving the meal she's prepared on the stove, the children are hungry, the slightest thing will launch hostilities. Marie puts off suppertime as long as she can, hoping that Romain will eat at the same time they do. Why bother? Every night, unable to take it any longer, she feeds the children before he comes in. During those few minutes of calm when the children are at the table, Marie drinks the port that Romain has brought her — it's more feminine than Scotch, he pointed out — to which she's had to resign herself, the bottle of Scotch having moved.

Often Marie tries to reverse this ordering of the world from which she's excluded. "Why don't you invite him for supper? Or at least have your Scotch in here instead of the garage!" In vain. Romain goes on thinking that Thomas is part of a world that belongs only to him, definitely not to the tribe.

Nor does Thomas complain about the order of the world. When his muscles are tired, when his back, his arms are working, pushing their strength to the limit, his head asks for nothing better. Not because it's empty, but because it is filled with calculations, soil enrichment, locations with maximum sunlight — so full there's no room left for anything else. It's good, he doesn't spend all day brooding over the obvious: there is no future for him in Rimouski. He was wrong, it's not here that he'll make a fresh start. It will be elsewhere. Maybe. And since he doesn't yet have any idea of what the shape of that elsewhere will be, the summer he has created for himself with his hands in the earth and in Rex's coat, his cool nights in the cellar, suit him perfectly.

Thomas wants the garden he's creating to be spectacular. Because it is the only trace that he'll leave of his stay in this town. For while he does not yet know what life has in store for him, he's quite certain that he will never set foot here again. A legacy, an offering, insurance for the future in case what comes next turns out badly, or not at all. A garden that will say day after day, year after year, that a person has done something in his life. But that's not the only reason. This garden is to thank Romain. Because if he hadn't brought him onto his property, Thomas would still be wondering whether Rimouski has any other living creatures aside from his deaf, blind dog, faithful companion in all his anxieties, those rediscovered or tenacious, along with those gone forever.

Yvonne's daily presence has made Marie lighter. But hasn't given her the keys to paradise. While her days aren't so heavy, they seem to her just as empty. Even more so ever since outside, close by, a man she knows seems to have found his own garden of Eden. The fervour that Thomas puts into his work is visible from kilometres away.

One morning Thomas knocks on the kitchen door. Yvonne is upstairs, following Romain's advice to the letter: to make the children disappear from their mother's field of vision now and then. Marie freezes briefly, surprised to see him on the steps.

"Come in," she says, trying unsuccessfully to hide her surprise.

"No thanks, I'll get your kitchen dirty," replies Thomas, smiling.

His clothes are muddy, his hair dishevelled too. His body scrawny, his arms too long. He is swimming in a sweater the colour of wet sand. His lopsided shoulders, his luminous, nearly childlike gaze.

It's only when the children are there that Marie intimidates Thomas. As if being a mother confers on her a title that commands respect. Aside from that, Marie is a young woman, neither beautiful nor ugly, lacking confidence and filled with an anger that she thinks she conceals brilliantly.

"I have a splitting headache. Do you have any Aspirin?"

"The doctor's office is next door!"

Marie said whatever popped into her mind, the first remark that came to her, caught on the fly. The opposite of what she wanted to say. Her usual defence mechanism when she feels she's been caught unawares.

Marie's rejoinder makes Thomas feel uncomfortable.

"Oh come on, I was kidding, you were right to come here," she says with a silly little laugh.

"That's what I thought," replies Thomas, reassured. "I'd scare Romain's patients and Madame Beaurivage. A scarecrow in the waiting room!"

Marie rummages in a cupboard. Runs water till it's cold.

"One or two?"

"Two."

"Is it bad?"

"I'm used to it. Headaches are second nature for me."

"Have you seen a doctor?"

"Too many. That's the problem actually. Let's say they're the aftermath of the war, there's nothing to be done."

He holds his hands out to Marie to take the glass and the pills. Thomas's dirty hands. The left one, into its palm Marie drops the strikingly white Aspirins, the right one clasping in its long fingers with soil-caked nails the glass of clear water.

Thomas's hands. At this precise moment the centre of everything.

Marie would like to take his rough, hardened hands in her own and bring them to her face, to smell them. Odour of humus, of roots and leaves mixed with that of his skin.

Thomas's dirty hands. That touch no one. That no one touches.

Marie tries to keep him there.

"You work hard, it's going to be gorgeous."

"Come and see me in a little while, Romain wants you to choose the plants for the borders."

"I don't know a thing about flowers!"

"Tomorrow I'll bring you a book with pictures of flowers and shrubs. It will give you some ideas."

Thomas hands her the glass, thanking her, and goes back to work. Tomorrow, thinks Marie, he'll be here again tomorrow.

A big book on the kitchen table. Yvonne has just put it there.

"Thomas gave me this for you." Another day begins. With its shouts of happy children, its still hesitant light in the house. With the strong, clear voice of Yvonne ruling over the world. With Romain's hands squeezing Marie's waist, his breath on her neck: "Good morning, try to enjoy yourself a little today. Why not drop in on your mother?" Another day. She'll have to remember to thank heaven for the fruit on the table, for the salty mildness of the air, for the insistent way that happiness insists on taking root in this home.

He didn't bring the book himself. Marie, her impatient movements, like an insult to life.

At the next table, our opposite number: two couples, flawlessly dressed. The one difference, they're in their thirties. I would have paid no attention if I hadn't noticed Joe's eyes on one of the young women. The kind of girl whose beauty leaves you speechless. She replied to Joe's gaze with a deceptively shy smile when she brought her glass to her lips, as if to say: "Okay, go ahead, you have my permission to admire me." Since then, Joe has been admiring her every five minutes. How many women have been knocked over by those blue eyes? I don't want to know. I've never been the only woman. I know that, I sense it. In spite of his love for me, and his loyalty, Joe isn't the type who'll resist. He's had so many opportunities, he's travelled so much. I've always imagined him with a double life: the loving husband and the guy who hangs out in terminals picking up girls.

It was so much easier not being jealous. Every time Joe left me for his business, he disappeared, no longer existed. He was a runaway in a sense. If I hadn't recognized his right to oblivion, I'd have been out of my depth, I'd have questioned my own existence. The freedom of the runaway is absolute. When he came home, when his extreme presence, his heat, his smell were given back to me, I would sometimes spend whole nights not sleeping so as not to waste even one second of the tremendous giddiness in which that body bound me.

This restaurant. This festive evening. Joe and the girl at the next table. A game that won't go any further. She's probably used to it, it must happen to her all the time. She has not yet felt this thing swoop down on her. The power of attraction, the law of gravity, the solemn law of falling bodies, of sagging flesh, insidious at first with the arrival of the forties, then, over time, more and more. Tonight, no man is looking at Hélène, our guest. No man is looking at me either.

What is Joe thinking about when his eyes meet the girl's? Maybe he's hoping that she'll leave before him so she won't see him stand and pick up his cane, maybe he thinks with bitter disappointment — or even despair — that more than ever, the game won't go beyond the premise of such a look. Or maybe he's not thinking of anything. For the moment, he is drinking, laughing at our friends' conventional jokes, but now it's not his loud, clear laughter from before; the paralysis has left marks — a fixed grin in which bitterness can be seen.

*Y*es, she will give in to the pressure of Romain and Yvonne. She will visit her mother. She won't take the car, will go on foot, won't use the sidewalk, will cut across the property. If she has decided to go out, it's not to take a fresh look at things or to get away from the boys or to see her mother. It's to be with him. Just five minutes under the trees between the mounds of cool earth. All alone with him. "I'm crazy," she murmurs at the mirror as she pins up her hair. Marie kisses the boys, she has gone to the trouble of doing her hair and putting on makeup. Has chosen clothes that she doesn't wear often. Romain will be pleased. Yvonne's daily report will be positive.

He doesn't hear her arrive. In the grass her high heels make her walk like a bird. It's Rex who tells Thomas that Marie is there — he's smelled her perfume — he lets out a moan, followed by an attempted growl that he muffles right away, Thomas having forbidden any atavistic behaviour on this territory.

Marie is holding her purse against her. Thomas smiles at her, glad that she's come. Marie's discomfort melts away at the sight of the little wrinkles filled with earth that appear at the corners of his eyes. "How's it going?" asks Marie. Thomas gives her the answer he would give to Romain, Yvonne, or any other passerby. He explains, describes in gardener's language the satisfaction he gets from turning over a small clump of stubborn clay, from overcoming obstinate roots, from being solely responsible for the state of grace he obtains from the sensation of his hands in the freshly loosened earth. "Maybe I'm becoming a happy idiot," he declares by way of conclusion.

"You should give me the recipe. I'd like to be one too," Marie laughs. "You see, in my opinion, the hardest thing is not being an idiot or happy, we all are at some time or other, no, it's always being the two that strikes me as complicated."

"We get there by practising."

"You should give me lessons."

"Gardening lessons?"

"No, lessons in becoming a happy idiot!"

"Oh! Well, it's the same thing!"

Before she leaves, Marie makes Thomas promise that he will guide her in selecting the flowers and plants. She'll come back to see him with the book he lent her. Marie has her revenge. She will come tomorrow herself. She won't do her errands via Yvonne.

The next day. The day after that. Every day, a mid-afternoon break to see Thomas. A few minutes, rarely longer, time for a Coke or a lemonade. The first times they remain standing, Marie leaning against a tree, Thomas holding onto his shovel or his fork. Then one afternoon the wooden crates appear, the same as the ones Romain and Thomas sit on for their six o'clock Scotch. Marie likes to think that he brought them so that she'd stay longer. It's the kind of thought she has to cultivate in order to reach her goal. Because it's not so easy to become a happy idiot, though Marie doesn't give up hope.

Every day the scene does not escape Romain. Around three o'clock he turns his head towards the window for a few seconds, rarely longer. Slightly jealous. Thomas and Marie, really? The thought doesn't even cross his mind. Simply jealous that one can drop everything in the middle of the afternoon just like that and sit on a crate, offer one's face to the late-June sun, thinking of nothing but what kinds of roses to plant or the reproductive cycle of butterflies. Above all, not about the results of examinations and the gloomy prognoses that he will have to pass on in two minutes to the couple and their sick child who have just come into the office. It's at six o'clock that his turn will come. The hour for the wooden crate, the Scotch, the sun on his face. The hour to be a happy idiot.

Little by little there settles between Thomas and Marie the confidence, the certainty that the other won't be a traitor. That words, for once, will not in any way constitute evidence against the other. They don't talk about themselves, not yet, but they've left the territory of horticulture to approach their own. Now Marie stays longer with Thomas. Sitting quietly on her crate, she watches him work. Often, they stop their conversation. Nothing is more soothing for Marie than this man with his tools, his silence, his pathetic work.

In the evening, Romain questions her with a look of feigned indifference.

"What did you talk about today?"

"Borders and shrubs."

Romain believes her, just as he believes every human being who sits down across from him, saying: "Doctor, I'm in pain."

One night Marie takes the initiative.

"Do you know the story about the statue of Saint John the Baptist in the cathedral at Chartres?"

"No," replies Romain, surprised, it's unlike Marie to bring up such a subject.

"On one of the facades of the cathedral," she continues, "there are statues, including one of Saint John the Baptist. Because it faces north, it's exposed to the sun's rays at just one moment of the year: on June 24, at five o'clock in the afternoon! It's incredible! And do you know what? That was planned while it was being built. In the thirteenth century! Isn't that incredible …"

"That story's a bit dubious, don't you think?" Romain replies.

"It's true, I assure you. There are even pilgrimages on that day, at five o'clock on the dot, to see the sun's rays on the statue. Thomas read about it in some kind of encyclopedia that deals with the main Christian saints."

"Thomas is interested in the lives of the saints?"

"No, but when he was in the asylum, that was the kind of book they gave him when he asked for something to read."

"He told you that?"

Marie detects a hint of annoyance in Romain's voice. Then she understands: Romain is competing with her for Thomas. It's not the ray of sunlight on a statue that matters in this story, it's the fact that she has had access to a small particle of Thomas, and it's to Romain, not Marie, that he should have mentioned reading in the hospital. Because that's the beginning Romain is waiting for, and after the first confidence would come another, more inviting, and then others. He's the one, after all, who is trying to make Thomas talk.

In the silence that follows, which they try to justify by the fact that their mouths are full and their attention is drawn by the children who are running around the table, each hears what the other says and what can be summed up in the same four words: Thomas belongs to me.

A short distance away, near the picture window that looks out on the river, an old couple is having dinner alone together. Their slowness, their silence. The waiter is particularly attentive to them, they must be regulars. Joe and me in fifteen years.

Or my parents today.

When a child disappears, does the family explode into a thousand shreds, or does it knit itself together so as to fill the space the child had occupied? What has become of my brothers? Given their ages — on the verge of being able to fend for themselves — and their attachment to me, my departure must have seemed like an earthquake, a shock wave, the feeling of having lived through something exceptional, then you pick up the pieces, rebuild, everything's back to normal. The event has become a lasting souvenir that their children will describe to their friends. But my parents — did they survive the upheaval?

I can't picture them as an elderly couple like the one at the table by the picture window. They separated shortly after I disappeared. Already my departure had left them on their own. Bernard and François, my older brothers, were away at school and no longer lived at home from September to May. André was about to join them. Had I stayed I would have spent a number of years alone with the two of them.

Perhaps my father would have left with the woman my brothers suspected of being his mistress. A year before I left they had created a whole novel around a secret affair between my father and a young woman. The fable had started one evening around seven o'clock, when François and Bernard had seen my father leave the hospital with a woman. They had walked quickly to the car and got in. My brothers turned it into a drama. André, who hadn't witnessed the scene and who was naturally pragmatic, cast himself as the devil's advocate: the flimsiness of the evidence prohibited such an assumption. Of course, I would never have been let in on the secret if André hadn't told me the whole story. In spite of what drove us apart, we got along well. His position in the family was ambiguous. He was definitely on the side of the boys, but there was just a year and a half between us, and a bond that I didn't understand at the time brought us together, perhaps reluctantly. Today, that bond is perfectly clear: he and I had been babies at the same time. We were together during the time of extreme childhood. If I had to see a single member of the family again, I would choose him. No, not exactly. He's the one I would choose to see before the others.

The story could have ended there. But my brothers saw my father with that woman again. They were leaving a building downtown. That time, André was with them. When he came home he knocked on my bedroom door right away. He seemed to be as incredulous as he was upset. I asked questions: Were they touching one another? Were they holding hands? Did they look like lovers? No, replied my brother, they looked like a couple leaving a building.

I remember the uneasiness that swept over us. There was not much more than the evening meal that brought us all together. And even then ... Most of the time one of them was absent. But not during the days that followed these incidents. My parents must have thought us strange. At mealtimes we didn't talk, we observed them, watching for a sign that would confirm my brothers' suspicions. One night I dared say to André: "Anyway, it wouldn't be surprising, poor Papa, she's so dry with him, like she is with everybody for that matter!" My brother was indignant. Not surprisingly, our respective Oedipus complexes didn't have the same target. The story died on the order paper, we never talked about it again.

Did my father look at women the way Joe is looking at this young beauty tonight? In my mind, as in my brothers', it was absolutely certain that my parents were no longer in love. We'd always known. But it didn't really matter. They were parents, after all, *our* parents, before they were a couple.

My father seemed unaffected by the situation. Always true to form, moderate in all things, never any anger or great outpourings. He loved us, he was above all a family man. He and my brothers were powerfully connected. Between him and me there was a distance despite the certainty of love. There was a zone of mystery between us that he didn't allow me to cross. For a long time I thought it was because I was a girl. But no, there was something else, a misunderstanding, an ache, a silence that separated us as much as it prevented too much distance between us. I was so angry with my mother, the main cause of all the ills on Earth, with her icy words, her absent looks, her nerve pills. She alone could be the family's rotten fruit.

We're so upfront at the age of fifteen.

All these memories resurfacing: I should have got drunk tonight. I never should have left Chicago.

The old couple got up. Slowly, with dignity, they made their way to the exit. When they went past us the old man brushed against my arm. He turned around, apologized with a smile. A tidal wave lifted me, carried me away, and threw me for a moment into my father's arms.

I don't feel well, I'm shaking, I'm suddenly cold to the bones. Joe leans towards me, I see him through a halo of mist.

"Lou, are you okay?"

I jump.

"I'd like to go now."

He leans again, wraps his arm around me, kisses me on my neck. An endless kiss. Maybe not endless, but in any case long enough for me to calm down and regain my self-confidence. Long enough for me to revel in my silly little victory: the stunning young thing at the next table has taken it all in. What do I care then if Joe has lived a life parallel with ours? His breath on my neck, his passionate presence. At every homecoming, at every moment. Whatever we don't see does not exist. Every runaway knows that.

*I*t was written in the sky or in the neatly symmetrical mounds of earth that now stand between the maples and the sidewalk. Marie and Thomas have just cast off. Between them from now on there will be no more garden, only their own truth snatched day by day from the temptation of silence.

Marie has led Thomas back some years to the very end of his internment, when he was taking newcomers under his wing. Terrified, bewildered by the crazy world in which they'd just been caged, they found in Thomas's eyes the infinitesimal thread of light to which they must cling to get through the day. They followed him, obedient children, into the hospital's vast vegetable gardens. Thomas showed them patiently how to weed or pick. They felt that it was to him and no one else that they owed their salvation. Thomas felt uncomfortable but content.

Marie, her childlike, often brutal way of tackling things. Her ill-considered rejoinders that she rejects as soon as she's said them.

"Know what you look like, with one shoulder lower than the other?"

She doesn't wait for Thomas's reaction.

"One of the boys, the middle one," she says — Marie never refers to her sons by name in front of Thomas, as if she wants them to exist less powerfully in his presence — "has a puppet that the older one tried to wreck, out of spite. Which resulted in one arm completely dislocated that hangs from one shoulder by a thread. He won't let me sew it back. He's adamant about keeping it in his bed, hidden under a blanket. It's a musical puppet that you wind up with a little key on the back."

"So it's a monster! Thanks a lot," he says, he mocks, feigning outrage.

"That's not what I meant!"

"I realize that, I'm getting to know you. Did your mother never tell you to think twice before you open your mouth? Look," he went on, turning his back, "I don't have a key ..."

"I find it so hard to say what I mean, I'm sorry. You bring your hand to your shoulder so often it seems painful. Since we first met I've been dying to know what happened to you and I don't dare ask."

"What happened to me? What happened to me?" he repeats, his voice suddenly unsteady.

He drops his shovel and sits on the crate next to Marie. The question is so broad. Like the river, like the sky. Broad as life when the knots are untied. Broad as the space between them that, without realizing it, they are trying to eliminate.

"My collarbone was broken twice."

"Twice! How did that happen?"

"Shock treatments."

Thomas pauses. He has never gone past those words. With anyone. Marie's face is so insistent, so familiar all at once. She hasn't moved back, hasn't looked away, hasn't changed the subject. Rex senses Thomas's embarrassment, stands with his muzzle on the man's knees.

For a fraction of a second, time stops. Marie, Thomas, Rex. A refuge, a high-security wing, a family.

"Go on," Marie murmurs.

"Shock treatments often cause injuries. The convulsions are intense. It's as if your own body is beating itself up. The muscle contractions are so violent — you can't imagine. My shoulder was injured. The muscles were torn, the bone broke. Then a few months later, when it was healing, my shoulder gave out again during a session. The muscles were torn again, in the same places, the fracture too. That time it was badly joined together and that's why I look like a puppet, as you say."

"Did you have a lot of shock treatments?"

"Enough to stop counting."

On the sidewalk in front of them, an old man walks hesitantly, stops, catches his breath, then turns onto the small cement lane that leads to Romain's office. Cars are driving along the street. The voices of children playing. Birds singing. The Earth has not emptied to leave Thomas and Marie alone for a moment.

At breakfast the next day, Joe is ready and waiting for me. He drank, I'm hungover. I have to say, I didn't give him a chance to play shrink last night. When we came home he looked after the dogs, I went straight to bed. He sobered up by himself, in front of the TV. Oh, but this morning he wants to know, he insists. He is breaking a pact between us. In the beginning, when we first met, he'd made a good try to find out everything: why I'd run away and from whom. I refused his request, bluntly and fiercely. If he wanted to keep me, he would have to regard me as a strange and unique creature, who one fine sunny morning had suddenly appeared in the Toronto terminal. The rest was none of his business, it belonged to me, it was my job. And I was going to make it. In fact I'd just proven it by being born in the midst of the crowd and the sound of trains, I would be able to put my memory to sleep and arrange things so that it wouldn't wake up for a hundred years. Joe had no choice but to accept that law of silence.

It all worked like a dream, the way I wanted, except that a hundred years isn't nearly as long as you might think.

Joe asks no questions, just sits there over his coffee with his arms folded. At his feet, the dogs. All three stare at me intensely. And tenderly. They have all the time in the world.

"Hang on, I'm going to get something," I say finally, getting up from my chair, relieved to no longer feel their eyes on me.

I don't fully understand what's happening. I'm the one who is getting ready to break the pact. Impossible this time to say no to Joe: on my neck I have the print of an endless kiss by a living man.

At the sight of the photo I've just put down in front of him, Joe is taken aback. He smiles ironically.

"Wow! Did you see them again?"

"No."

"Are you going to?"

"I don't know. I really don't know."

"When was this photo taken?"

"In 1957. I was one year old."

"Is that your grandmother holding you?"

"No, it's the maid."

"I see. So the young lady has a nursemaid!" he says, then bursts out laughing.

He's won. The whole morning will be devoted to the auto-biographical tale of Louise Lemieux, alias Lou Thompson.

When I'd finished, Joe said: "If I hadn't accosted you in Toronto, maybe you'd have been on the first bus home. You actually just ran away for a few hours and then I kidnapped you!"

"Not at all, I was willing. If a person agrees to go away with someone, it isn't a kidnapping."

"But you were such a little girl."

A slight pause, a slight uneasiness between us. He's right. Aside from taking the bus, I didn't decide anything. The rest of the story belongs to him.

"So when will you see them again?" he asks, as if to challenge me.

"The only person I miss is Yvonne. She must have been dead now for ages."

"You aren't answering my question."

"I know."

I missed Yvonne long before my departure. After the death of her mother, whom she'd lived with and taken care of, she moved into the house. That was a few weeks before I was born. She used to say that it was the most beautiful day of her life. She was the opposite of my mother: strong, organized, cheerful. How did she manage to look after everything? Four very young children, the meals, the upkeep of the house, which was enormous.

I owned Yvonne. And belonged to her in turn. My refuge, my rampart, my most reliable ally against my brothers' teasing and dirty tricks. I stuck to her like a burr. When my youngest brother started school, I was in heaven for two years, having her all to myself. Until it was my turn to be plucked out of the nest by school. We had created a small, closed universe. We let no one in. Anyway, who would have wanted in? Not my brothers, who saw Yvonne first and foremost as an old lady out of step with reality, though she was kind. My mother left us alone. Long before being the daughter of Marie and Romain, I was Yvonne's.

I saw her cry twice. On the day my mother told her that she'd hired a cleaning lady. A young woman. Yvonne had just turned sixty-nine. She could no longer do all the work. The cooking, the sewing, the children — I was around ten — would still be her domain. The rest would go to the new woman. Yvonne began to sob quietly, trying desperately to swallow her tears. My mother became a little impatient.

"Really, Yvonne, you should be happy, I'm doing it for you!"

The new cleaning lady appeared the very next day; she came to the house twice a week. On those days Yvonne was transformed into a merciless majordomo. Poor girl! She put up with her orders and criticisms without ever answering back.

I saw Yvonne cry again five years later, a year before I left. It had gone on for weeks. This time she wasn't the only one who cried, we were two. I had got wind of it before she did. I'd learned from my brothers to listen at doors, they often did it when they wanted something from my parents. A matter of warding off blows, of preparing irrefutable arguments, they said. On that we stuck together like musketeers. I didn't have to fear that they would tell on me. So I followed everything attentively: my mother's plan, my father's opposition, the tension, the conflict, and, finally, his surrender. My mother wanted to get rid of Yvonne. She didn't want to deal with an old woman, take care of her, because, she insisted, it was inevitable that Yvonne would eventually take sick. My mother said that her own best years were ahead of her. I was fifteen then, my brother François nineteen, in a few years we would both be gone. She wanted to enjoy her freedom. My father kept telling her that Yvonne had no one but us. My mother replied tirelessly that there are excellent homes for the elderly. It seemed clear to me that my father wouldn't win this battle. Their conversations left me without a doubt. I knew well my mother's brittle tone and her inflexibility. I had even tried to intervene. I'd gone to see my father at the hospital to confess that I knew everything and that I was on his side. I hoped that would give him a reason to stand up to my mother. "You have to understand her," he sighed, "you'll all be leaving home, I'm not there all that much, we can't impose Yvonne on her." He acquiesced, as always. Of course we had to understand her. It was an impossible mission. I was disappointed. At the end I said a terrible thing that made him turn white, that clenched his jaws — a sign of extreme annoyance in my father: "It's Mama who should be put in an institution, not Yvonne."

The weeks that followed were painful. I sided with the victims, next to Yvonne. My mother, with the tyrants, and between the two enemy camps, my father, in the camp of humanitarian aid. Yvonne left one fine morning. I was at school.

As if to prove to us that she'd been right, my mother launched into a campaign of seduction. The era of Yvonne was well and truly over. She changed all the kitchen utensils and the dishes. At mealtimes she presented us with unfamiliar food, cooked dishes we'd never tasted before. She waited for our compliments with an ingenuous look. My father and my brothers paid them. Especially my father. He fell for it like a child, returned her smiles. At times, from the way he looked at my mother, you'd have thought they were in love. I was absolutely furious. I only picked at my food. Later, in my room, I would stuff myself with cookies. I was no good at anorexia.

My mother seemed relaxed, we saw her sing, take an interest in what we did and said. This contented-domestic-goddess-in-the-bosom-of-her-happy-family regime lasted for two months, maybe three. Afterwards, life went back to normal.

I was faithful to Yvonne. I visited her as often as I could. After a while I had to acknowledge that I was disturbing her. Yvonne was beaming; I'd never seen her like that. She'd had her hair cut, she dressed nicely, wore cheap jewellery. She played cards, had started a knitting and sewing club, had become in a way the chief scout of the residence. She'd evaded both my predictions and papa's: she was better off without us, she was happier since she'd left the family.

*T*he July heat sneaks in without notice, until it has become oppressive. By noon, it's practically impossible to work in the sun. The body resists, pleads. Mornings, Thomas arrives even earlier than before, and he leaves the garden at the beginning of the afternoon. He ends his day on the bank of the river or in the cool cellar with Rex. It's not just the scorching heat that makes him back away. Marie, with her face straining towards him, her face, which he now thinks is beautiful, her pale eyes, her mouth, her questions that want to know everything. Romain's face too, the way he throws his head back when he drains his glass of Scotch. "How was your day, Thomas? And how was Marie, in a good mood?" A garden, a job that lasted for a summer, the loyalty of a deaf and blind old dog, that was all he'd hoped for, nothing else. Nothing that can place him beyond his depth or light a fire.

After two days of missed meetings, one morning Marie joins Thomas. No question now of sitting quietly on a crate. Romain wants her to participate in designing this garden, it will be good for her, raise her morale. The doctor has never been so right: the mere sight of Thomas wiping his forehead,

his smell of sweat, his willing and hunted gaze have an immed-
iate effect on Marie.

Stopped short, Thomas tries hard to separate things: Marie,
now, here, with him. Marie, elsewhere, later, with Romain and
the children. Watertight compartments, unshakeable ramparts.
Take advantage of it. Marie the companion he's never had.
Will never have. Want nothing but the present moment. They
are on their knees, facing one another. A mound of damp
earth between them. Marie has held her hand out, palm-up,
over the flower bed. Thomas drops seeds into it. They're phlox,
he explains to Marie, they're also called *Louise*, he doesn't
know why. He gathered the seeds last year on the Plains of
Abraham, where he was working. These flowers are prolific,
every year they reseed themselves. Marie won't have to look
after them. With time there will be more and more, the
clumps will get bigger. It will be spectacular, he promises.

A ritual. Marie drops the seeds one by one into the fur-
rows that Thomas has just made.

"I feel as if I'm playing like a child," says Marie, breaking
the religious silence they had etched upon their movements.
"It's funny," she went on, "you, I can imagine as a child, but
not Romain. He's so reasonable, so well turned-out. No, I
really can't imagine him any other way. But you knew him
then. What was he like?"

"I can't tell you."

"Come on! Did Romain swear you to professional secrecy?"
she replies, laughing.

"No, I don't remember."

"I don't understand," replies Marie, the smile on her face in suspense.

"You know, memory is like shoulders, shock treatment can break it too. Pieces get lost, disappear. You do what you can to get them back, but nothing works. Yes, I remember my childhood. But it's vague, except for certain precise events: Christmas *réveillons*, punishments at school, Saturdays in my father's warehouses — that kind of memory, you see; but Romain is nowhere in those memories, I can't place him."

"But ... but that means that you don't know us! We're strangers to you!"

"That's right."

"Why didn't you say anything before?"

"When a guy comes home after a five-year absence, three of them spent in an asylum, when he sees his father and his childhood friend waiting for him at the station, it's not in his interest to confess to his memory lapses."

"Do you intend to tell Romain?"

"No. What difference would it make? I haven't lied or betrayed anyone. I haven't profited from a situation. I was acting in good faith. I thought that by rubbing shoulders with him I'd get back that missing piece of my life. Time passes and nothing resurfaces. It doesn't matter now; it would have if I'd wanted to stay. But since I intend to go back to Quebec City at the end of summer ... After I finish the garden, in fact. And I believe that Romain has friendly feelings for me.

If I told him the truth I'd risk becoming a patient, and I don't want to be anybody's patient anymore."

They go back to work in silence. Marie could savour her victory. There is more between Thomas and her now than there will ever be between Romain and Thomas. It's still not enough.

*T*hat evening in the restaurant marked a turning point for Joe. He re-established ties with what he loved in the world: possible encounters, crowds, activity. He knew that the small amount he'd glimpsed of it that night could be multiplied by ten, by a hundred, in Chicago, New Delhi, or Rio. I kept telling him that he had the gods on his side. No, he replied, I don't believe in the gods or in God, I was accompanied by fairies. We're always better off with women! For the reality was blindingly obvious. For some time now his physical condition had been improving. He'd put on weight and muscle, he walked with confidence. His mouth was no longer twisted when he talked, the words flowed more readily. All efforts were less arduous. It was as if that outing to the restaurant had been the most effective cure. Since then, spending the day glued to his screen no longer satisfies him. He has to move. He paces the beach, walks the dogs. Yesterday morning he asked me what winter was like here. I dared not give him a clear picture. I said nothing about the intensity of the cold, about night falling at four o'clock, about ice floes like a vise, about the feeling of confinement.

Now that he is busy being reborn, he leaves me alone with my moods. Which doesn't stop him from scratching the wound now and then: How old are your parents now? When you go to Rimouski do you ever walk past your childhood home? Joe's questions. He thinks that he's sly.

The house. When I have to go to Rimouski I take detours to avoid temptation. At night though, when I can't get to sleep, I go back there constantly. Not to reclaim life in a family, but to resume possession of the premises. I visit it, I become the resident ghost. I inspect it, I search it all the way into its infinite nooks and crannies. I wander outside too: I reappropriate the garden, the garage. Once I've visited the entire estate, I begin again. Like Sisyphus, I'm unsuccessful. There's always one detail that escapes me: a knick-knack, a piece of furniture, the colour of a rug or a curtain.

My memories resemble the mammoths discovered in glaciers. Thirty years of freezing have left them intact. I can see everything as if I were there. My brothers' bedrooms, genuine shambles, drove Yvonne crazy; my parents' room, spare, incomparably clean — I didn't feel comfortable there, the decor was so frozen, and then all the rest — the kitchen, the two sitting rooms, one upstairs, the other in the base-ment, living places where the tribe got together, carefree, enraged, exuberant, silent, despairing, depending on the days, but always totally ignorant of the future.

"Do you go past the family house?" That damned question of Joe's is running through my head. If I don't go now, I'll have to wait for six months. Because as soon as the snow falls it will be impossible. Already we feel as if we're under a suspended sentence. As if heaven has granted us a favour. For a week now it's been cold. "Too cold," says Joe, surprised. Overhead, big clouds threaten but don't burst. The north wind won't let go. The river's anger flows all the way to us, its waves pound the beach with regular shocks, raging, disfiguring it. Around the house the ground is frozen. The beach tries to defy the assaults. Joe and the dogs support it with their presence. I refuse to stick my nose outside. Joe is surprised again: "Are you painting clouds now?" When the sky overflows, the snow will take us without transition to another universe. Which is why time is short, because it's not the house that interests me most, it's the garden. Now I regret not having gone there before. I could have seen its August splendour, it would have been better than today, one should never look at a garden in November. It's impossible to imagine its beauty when it is overrun with desolation.

All at once, with no warning, the sky is torn apart like the Red Sea. The beautiful, warm light of the sun restores colours. With any luck, I'll get there before the sky closes again.

$\mathscr{R}$omain is cursing the heat wave, which afflicts old people and babies. House calls are multiplied. When he finally comes in at night, also exhausted by the heat, he can no longer take refuge in the garage with Thomas for their Scotch break; in the house, the children are sullen, it's so hot that they can't get to sleep, they howl in unison, sometimes until eleven o'clock at night; Marie is elusive, absent-minded, disconnected, as if she no longer lives in the house, as if she is no longer the keystone. "It's too hot, we have to get out of here, the sooner the better," Romain says to Marie one night.

A colleague has offered him his seaside summer house not too far away to the east. A beach for the boys, the sea wind, cool nights. Three weeks. Yvonne would come to be with Marie for a while. He would spend a few days at the beginning, he could even join them some evenings after work. In the meantime, Thomas could move into the house.

The verdict falls on Marie like a prison sentence.

She calculates: they leave in one week's time. Thomas goes back to Quebec City when the garden is finished. One week's respite plus a three-week absence — how much time will there be when they return? And time for what? To prove once and for all that life made a mistake by confining her in a big house with three babies; time for her to become embedded in Thomas's memory and never leave it; time for Thomas's dirt-covered hands to be placed on her body; time for Thomas's madness to be lost in her, to melt into her own. This time, it has to happen. Afterwards, she swears, everything will go back to normal. She will be a patient town rebuilding itself after a fire. A discreet town on a river.

Marie grumbles.

"There's so much to do and we haven't even left yet! If that's what *vacation* means, I'd just as soon do without!"

"No, no, you'll see, we just have to make a small effort so that we can enjoy it more."

Yvonne and Marie busy themselves with the preparations. They need to think of everything. Boxes and suitcases pile up in the living room. "It looks as if we're moving!" The car can't hold everything, so Romain will make a first run with their supplies: Yvonne cooks food for the first days, she'll bring more when she joins Marie and the children. Already this morning, before breakfast, Yvonne was at work.

"We aren't going into the woods, there are grocery stores outside Rimouski!" jokes Romain.

"We know what has to be done!" Marie snaps.

Yvonne and Romain exchange a knowing look.

Outside, it is raining. Thomas has been away for two days. How does he manage, Marie wonders, not to come, how can he waste this time that he could be spending with me? Wake up, Marie, wake up, cries a little voice deep inside her, can't you see that you're all alone in this story, all alone in this madness?

The big day. The boys are excited though they don't know why. Romain whistles non-stop. Yvonne runs around in every direction. The weather is gorgeous. A while ago Thomas brought his travel bag to the kitchen. He asked Marie if Rex's presence in the house bothered her.

"Of course not."

They exchanged a silent smile.

"In three weeks I have a hunch you'll have finished your work," Marie added, emphasizing *three weeks* more than necessary.

"If the weather's on my side, it's quite possible."

"Too bad, I'd have liked to be there. I must admit I've come to enjoy gardening."

"Oh, there'll be lots for you to do! You haven't finished with that garden."

"I'm not afraid of hard work."

Platitudes. That's all they can come up with. Marie bites her lips.

On the doorstep Yvonne and Thomas respond to Romain's broad waves. Each of them hopes for his portion of miracle from this vacation. Romain hopes it will bring back Marie's smile, Thomas that it will take it away from him, Marie that it will pass quickly.

Marie was expecting a chalet. Luxurious, yes, but a chalet. It is a vast house on a small cliff that looks out on the sea. A narrow road winds its way to a beach that is circled by rocks. A perfect lawn around the house offered up to the wind.

They settle in right away. There's a place for all their belongings here, they are at home. Romain looks after everything with an enthusiasm that disarms Marie. Do not disappoint, she repeats to herself.

One might say that they've all joined in to send her straight to hell. The boys have never been so amusing; the baby doesn't demand his mother's attention at every moment. Romain is relaxed, as if he's been set free from another version of himself. He actually forgets to shave. Marie and Romain spend long moments on the terrace facing the sea, doing nothing but watch the children play. At five o'clock they bring out the Scotch, the afternoon drags on. Here, the explosive hours don't exist: the boys take their meals and their baths without protesting, they go to sleep early, exhausted by their day in the fresh air. When it is their turn to eat, Romain stuffs himself, Marie nibbles. Their conversations revolve around trivial details, sometimes Marie bursts out laughing. At night she responds to Romain's desire, successfully hiding her lack of enthusiasm. He thinks he's won the game, that it was simple in the end, that he should have thought of it before. Women like his wife pass through his office every day. They sit up straight on their chairs. They try to be stoical, but after a minute tears spring to their eyes. They don't know how to put into words what is happening, they talk about fatigue, children, hard work. Romain prescribes tranquilizers or sleeping pills. What else can he do? But not to Marie. He has something better to offer her. What's more, he offers it to her.

Marie is alone only when Romain is finally asleep. She frees herself from his embrace, turns her back to him, and inhales deeply. It is the only moment when she can be with Thomas entirely. All through the day she has to share him. With the children's laughter, with Romain's breath on her neck, with the sound of waves on the rocks. All those forms of music bury Thomas's voice. Then she has to wait till night to hear it again. His voice and the rest. His shy gaze, his big body, his soil-covered hands. Marie talks to him, tells him that he's not the only burn victim wandering the streets of the city, that she is burning too, but in silence, in the still course of her arteries. Hell, she tells him again, can be nothing else: days at a time in a perfect illusion of happiness, the imposter wearing a light dress in the summer sun, she, Marie, surrounded by her dear ones, posing for posterity against the background of the sea and the blue sky. Unforgettable vacation. One day she will be old, faded, sick. In her mind, the memory of August 1955. Life will have passed — perhaps not sparing her, who can know? No one can read in her eyes, creased by the blinding light, no one can see the she-wolf spying on the gardener, who sees nothing but his plants. True madness is not to find the echo of one's own.

And so from deep in her night, Marie begs Thomas to answer her. Once, only once.

After the first four days, Romain announces that he won't be going back as planned. He has called Madame Beaurivage and asked her to cancel his appointments for the next three days. Things are going so well here and he wants to take advantage of it as much as possible. He tells Marie that it's fantastic, it gives him another two days of vacation. On the last day he will pick up Yvonne and bring her here, then he'll go back to Rimouski. After that, when he has resumed his work, he'll do his best to work shorter days, so that he'll be able to join them here some evenings. Not to mention Sundays.

It's not his enthusiasm that Marie remembers from his words, no, only a few words that change everything: in three days someone has to go and pick up Yvonne. She will go.

Thomas thought that he could make more progress without Marie's presence at his side. He wants to have finished when she returns. He feels that he's being pushed, as if a menace were hovering over him. On the contrary, though, he has slowed down. A migraine has him in its grip; he's been sleeping badly since he moved into the house. Rex is nervous too, he keeps bumping his head against the wall. They both miss their cellar. Thomas has promised Romain that he'll look after the house until they come home. Evenings, he lingers outside, sprawled on a chaise longue, head about to burst, doesn't go inside until night has fallen completely. He sleeps on the velvet sofa in the living room. No bed for him in this house. Mornings, he goes outside as soon as he can. This house causes him pain. In his head. A pain that he doesn't recognize. Everything here throws him back to his poverty: no wife, no child, no friend, no work, no house, no future — nothing but the present moment, which is hammering his skull. What will happen to him in three weeks' time? Each thing, each object in this house, increases his unrest. The bathroom is a torture chamber: Marie's perfumes, Romain's eau de cologne, the hairbrushes, nail scissors, the thick towels in which he buries his face. All those artifacts exist only to remind him that he owns nothing, that the red night has devastated everything, that it has never ended, that no city has been rebuilt in him, that he is simply used to living amid the devastation of the burned land. He had been told that one can make a fresh start, that one can rebuild his nest anywhere. No, it's not true, a man moves restlessly, turns over the earth, adds ashes, people say that it helps plants to grow. But nothing takes root.

To spare me, to tame the emotion that could submerge me, I travel along streets that were my teenage routes. My parents must not live here anymore. At seventy-four and seventy-eight, they're too old for such a big house. Very likely they've buried themselves in one of those deluxe condos along the river, slightly to the west. Assuming that they're still alive, or still together. Who will recognize this woman who in a few minutes will pace the sidewalk outside Doctor Lemieux's beautiful, big red-brick house? Impossible even to stare at this passerby who's hidden by her big, dark glasses, the bottom of her face buried in the mohair collar of her sweater.

At the last street corner, reality is spread out all at once. Provocative, scandalous.

First the house, its front door surmounted by an ochre awning that comes all the way out to the street. Then, planted on the lawn, a carved wooden sign adorned with gilded borders: *Inn — Fine Dining*. All the windows have been replaced, but the house has kept its affluent and mysterious style. My father's office has undergone the most significant changes. It's become a large living room, completely glassed-in. Small, low tables, comfortable chairs, plants. Guests probably have breakfast here, and pre-dinner drinks and after-dinner coffee.

What's scandalous is not that the house has become an inn. I'm quite pleased that one can go inside to eat, drink, and sleep in our childhood bedrooms. Anyway, the house is used to crowds: so many people have paraded before my father to cry out their pain, their distress. This then is a kind of revenge, which seems fair enough. The victory of pleasure over misery.

No, the shock comes from the garden. Two-thirds of it no longer exists, it's been turned into a parking lot for the inn. An excessively big parking lot. The final third, the closest to the house, is a lawn on which are scattered Muskoka chairs in groups of four. The perimeter of the garden has been preserved. Half of the maples that surrounded it have disappeared; some are in bad shape. A frame of lawn clasps the immense rectangle of grey asphalt, of which the monotony is broken by white lines to indicate individual parking spaces. At this hour of the day the parking lot is empty.

There's nothing left.

I wish that Joe were with me right now. He would say: "Come," pulling on my sleeve. We would walk towards the parking lot, and at the foot of a big maple, we would sit down. I would feel slightly cold. I would huddle up against him. "I've got a surprise for you," he would say, in French to make me happy. And from the big inside pocket of the old, leather bomber jacket that he thinks will last forever, he'll take a small flask of Scotch. I like Scotch. We would drink straight from the flask, in silence, in the thrifty sun of late afternoon. It would be a perfect moment. Then I would stare intensely at the asphalt so that the magic would begin to operate: a few minutes later it would change from grey to green, then one by one the shrubs, the flower beds, the garden furniture would emerge. By way of finale, the unique Marie, with her straw hat and her pastel apron, kneeling in front of her phlox. I would lead Joe in turn: "Come and meet your mother-in-law!" Slowly, we would walk towards her, I would grab Joe's hand, she would raise her head, on her face I would read: "Who are these strangers?"

A plan is always fragile. A house of cards. The slightest thing can overwhelm it. Marie is driving slowly. So far, everything has gone according to her wishes.

Romain thought it a good idea for her to pick up Yvonne. A day off, a day without the boys, could only do her good. Finally, he won't come home till evening, he'll take care of everything, give the children their bath, put them to bed. He wants Marie to have a perfect postcard memory of their family vacation.

Summer rejoices. Marie lets herself be carried along by the road, by the August sun that is summoning her to drive up the river to a man who's not expecting her. She has entrusted Romain with far more than their children, she has left him everything: her doubts, their youth, the past, the future — their own and the boys'. She has held on only to the next few hours, bare, warm hours that resemble a promise.

Marie is at once calm and restless. She is extremely attentive to the landscape that streams by, to the purring of the engine. A question of losing nothing. That moment will not come again. That certainty is already inscribed in every cell of her body: it will be the first time she has run away, and the last.

If Marie were to listen to herself, she would park at the end of the street. She would go to him on foot, he would be wrapped up in his work, he wouldn't look up till the last moment. When he saw her his face would light up. She would open her arms, Thomas would throw himself into them. It would be that simple. It's her favourite scenario. The only one she lets herself imagine.

Marie parks the car next to the garage. She closes the door without letting it slam. Thomas isn't in the garden. Marie goes inside, checks all the rooms, he's not in the house either. He is there though, Marie knows it, on the counter are some dirty dishes, and the screen door in the kitchen isn't locked. Marie goes back outside. Near a tree at the back of the garden, the zigzagging silhouette of Rex appears. Marie goes towards him, she'll find Thomas. In the space that separates her from him, she crosses it with a confidence that life, until this day, has never granted her, Marie sheds all her skins. Which drop one by one onto the ground like clothing being shed in haste. It is naked that she will appear before Thomas.

He's asleep in the shadow of a maple, his jacket folded under his head. His hot, damp strands of hair are stuck to his forehead. His hands nearly joined. You might think he was praying. With extreme gentleness, Marie approaches and sits down beside him. A moment later she bends over and places her lips on Thomas's hands. His hands that taste of earth. He opens his eyes. Above his face, Marie's. "Come, follow me," she murmurs. Slowly, side by side, they head for the house, as if they had all the time in the world. Which they do: from now on they are both outside memory.

Thomas's turn to lead her. The living room, the floral motifs in the plaster ceiling, the dark, polished woodwork, the heavy drapes, the dark-red velvet sofa.

The house, the city, the universe on fire.

Marie's red afternoon.

Marie is late. Yvonne is waiting for her on the sidewalk. With her baggage and heaps of provisions she has prepared.

"I was getting worried!" she says without a hint of reproach in her voice. Yvonne is clearly delighted. Holidays, real holidays, something she has never known.

In the car she prattles on and on. Marie listens with half an ear, at once relieved and surprised to appear intact. The paradox of secrets. Thomas. Not an inch of her skin that he hasn't touched. Thomas. Less than half an hour ago. Thomas. His smell, his mouth, his arms around her neck, his voice: "Leave now."

After she's run out of gossip, Yvonne is silent for a moment. Marie savours the pause. So much silence is necessary for keeping a secret.

"Anyway, Madame Marie, the week seemed awfully long with all of you gone. You can't imagine how much I missed my babies!"

At these words, a shudder passes through Marie's whole body. Dried semen on her thighs. Thomas's sex inside her. Romain's. "My babies," said Yvonne. The certainty of the womb, the only one a woman possesses.

～

THOMAS SPENDS HOURS SLUMPED in an armchair across from the velvet sofa. As he did when he was taken back to his room after a shock therapy session. Exhausted, broken. Despairing, yet miraculously healed. To be alive, to have survived.

Rex, for no apparent reason, starts to yelp. The world begins to turn again. Thomas tidies up the living room, the kitchen, hurriedly picks up his things. Romain must be already on his way.

In a few days' time Thomas will have finished his work. Of course there'll still be flowers and shrubs to plant. So much to do, a garden is never done. Next spring Marie will fill the empty spaces, she'll know how.

Romain comes back late that evening. Nothing has changed. Thomas was dreading the moment when he would see him again. Neither regrets nor remorse have come up. He doesn't look away when Romain talks about Marie and the vacation that has done them so much good.

Romain asks Thomas what he intends to do. Thomas replies that he'll return to Quebec City, that he'll have no trouble going back to his job. He will complete the season with his team of gardeners. He'll be glad to see them. During the winter he'll look for something better somewhere else. More complex gardens, tropical greenhouses. He wouldn't mind going out West or to the States.

"So we're liable not to see you for quite a while. Do you realize what you're leaving us?" says Romain, spreading his arms to indicate the vast property that is now a garden. "You see, it will be the living proof of our friendship, which has been so solid since childhood."

Thomas nods, as if in approval.

They fall silent. After a moment Thomas says, his voice choked: "I've got something important to deal with. I need your help."

Then, glancing in the direction of Rex, he lowers his voice.

"I can't take him with me. He'll have to be put to sleep."

At once, Romain's speech for the defence. "Why not leave him with us? He knows us, I'm sure he'll get attached to the children. He's an old dog, but he's not suffering, he's used to his handicap, you're always saying that! Give him his chance … We'll take good care of him, don't worry."

Of course, Thomas thinks, Romain can't react otherwise. Men's bodies, the bodies of their dogs. Beating hearts. Life against death. Never would he agree to back down.

And to prove what he has just suggested, Romain strokes Rex, who repays him by licking his hand. It's a done deal.

oe is someone my mother would have liked. Not the way he was at the beginning, no, the way he was a little later and today, with his money, his blue eyes, his wrinkles, his casual manner. Class! Except for his bomber jacket. It would have taken her no time to reproach him for it. Joe would have laughed, playing the innocent: "But it's a very fine bomber jacket!" I wouldn't have joined in, wouldn't have sided with Joe, I would have had a good laugh too. In the garden, when I joined my mother, there was no conflict between us. In that sacred place my mother was someone else. In the garden, I loved my mother.

Never would I have dared go to see her without knowing if it was one of her good or bad days. Yvonne possessed the answer. "Yes, pet, go ahead," or: "Oh, well, I need you in the kitchen, I can't manage on my own, sweetheart." I didn't insist. I was learning how to read between the lines.

When Yvonne gave me the green light, I would run and join my mother. I was very careful. I would kneel down beside her, but not too close. I would watch her hoe, sow, transplant without a word. If it was a really good day she would explain why she had to do this or that this way and absolutely not some other way. And, supreme fusion, she would hand me a tool so that I could garden too, or, even better, she'd let me water what she had planted. It was not so much our shared affection that was so precious to me at those moments, it was my mother's attitude towards herself: her relaxed attitude, her smile, the sensuality of her movements, her hands in the cool earth. In her garden, my mother was alive. During my teenage years I stopped joining her there. I'd taken a sudden dislike to the garden.

I thought that by leaving I was avoiding a danger. I was sure of it. I stuck out my chest: *I* had the courage to say no. No to what though? I couldn't explain it. When I see her like that again, bent over her flowers, fragile, absent, and at the same time terribly present, I can't help thinking that it really was a matter of life and death. If I had stayed, I would have started to hate her. Truly. For good.

For how long have I been transfixed in front of this parking lot? I didn't see a thing: the sky clouded over, the sun disappeared, the wind came up, the air is suddenly freezing.

Things happened while I wasn't there.

*I*n a while, after supper, Thomas will hand over Rex to his new masters. Tomorrow, he leaves. The only sign that marks the event: Thomas's mother serves roast beef, mashed potatoes, and peas. Menu exclusive to Sunday lunch after Mass, which Thomas does not attend. In the end they won't have been close together, Thomas having been absent most of the time or having taken refuge in the cellar. He reads their aging faces: awkwardness and relief. They will resume their quiet life. They won't miss Thomas, he won't miss them. They're even. Thomas only asked for one thing: the quilted tartan bedspread. For a fraction of a second his mother felt moved: "You want the bedspread from when you were a little boy!" Had Thomas a little hatred in him, he would have corrected her: "Not for me, for Rex."

Since it's been decided that his dog will go to Romain and Marie, Thomas has bought a collar and a leash. He thought that Rex would not submit easily. On the contrary, it simplified his life. Following the leash as it advances, pulled by a beloved hand, instills trust. They walk confidently at dusk, the man and the dog, neither one knowing what the future will be made of. Blind and deaf.

Thomas cannot possibly leave without seeing Marie. It's out of the question that he play the disgraceful role he'd played five years ago. No disappearance, no running away. He will stand upright before Romain and Marie. He has not proven himself unworthy. Everything he has experienced since his return has revolved around them. For each of them he nurtures the same affection. Only it has expressed itself differently. He is leaving them his treasure: a dog and a garden. Never in his entire life has he given so much.

He doesn't know in what state he'll find Marie. He simply wants her to understand that he bore her despair for the space of an afternoon. It's not much, but it is immense. Let her understand that he loves her, will always love her, but doesn't love her. In him, things coexist in all their contradictions, but most of all there's no room for anyone; he chose long ago to advance alone along his scorched road. Thomas prefers to see her with Romain present. Just in case. A hitch, yes. Maybe, in a sense, he's running away. Marie's reprimands or her caresses. Her excesses. Her ruined look. Take no risks.

Again and for the last time, Thomas is in the kitchen. It's too dark now for the three of them to go outside together and salute the garden by way of farewell. Marie has spent time in the sun during her holidays. Her skin is golden, her voice expressionless. She is sitting opposite Thomas. Her face is inscrutable, as it is on her bad days. Thomas doesn't want to linger. He gives them instructions about Rex. Romain pokes fun.

"Hey, you sound like Marie talking to Yvonne when she looks after the children!"

"Okay, I guess that's it," says Thomas, getting up.

Romain, his handshake, his embrace, his straightforward expression. Marie, Thomas's discreet kiss on her cheek. Her drowned eyes.

The last embrace is for Rex. Thomas wraps his arms around him, buries his face in his neck. "Forgive me, old friend." Final image, final sad smile of Thomas, who shuts the door behind him. Silence in the kitchen. Only Rex lets out a plaintive little moan.

*I*t's dark when I come back. Joe asks me where I was. I answer him with my most beautiful smile. We curl up on the sofa in front of the patio doors. It's time for Scotch.

"Now the show can begin!" I say, raising my glass as if for a toast.

A few minutes later the sky bursts, furious gusts of snow, a howling wind. The dogs, anxious, break the prohibition: they jump onto the sofa, lie curled up between us. The universe suddenly shrinks, it's warm, cozy. An ark, a rampart against every storm.

Our silence.

Time stops. It seems to me that we haven't moved from the sofa since that night in November. As we look on, winter rages non-stop: snow, fog, freezing rain, northeast wind, roads shut down or icy. Not one week goes by that it doesn't deal us some blow. Like some furious person who's taking revenge.

Gradually the river has pulled back. Now it's only a thin blue ribbon on the horizon at the end of the ice field.

"Will this last very long?" Joe asks me one night as he swallows his Scotch.

"It will be around for a good while yet, you know, it's just the beginning of February."

A few days later he tells me, "You know what I'm thinking about? A house, with huge fenced-in grounds for the dogs."

"Isn't that what we have here? And without a fence?"

"Yes, but in Illinois, winter's not so long or so fierce ..."

With those words, dizziness, nerves, euphoria, itching muscles, the uncontrollable need to leave. To run away one more time. I burst out laughing, bringing Joe along with me. In the end I think the dogs are laughing with us too.

"There'll be a garden, a real one, with flowers. At night we'll drink Scotch while we watch the sunset."

"Whatever you want, baby, whatever you want."

The production of the title *After the Red Night* on Rolland Enviro 100 Print paper instead of virgin fibres paper reduces your ecological footprint by :

Tree(s) : 4
Solid waste : 103 kg
Water : 9 760 L
Suspended particles in the water : 0,7 kg
Air emissions : 227 kg
Natural gas : 15 m^3

100%

PERMANENT

Printed on Rolland Enviro 100, containing 100% post-consumer recycled fibers, Eco-Logo certified, Processed without chlorinate, FSC Recycled and manufactured using biogas energy.